"Were You with Hercules?" Demetrios Demanded.

"It's none of your affair whether I was or not," Helen rebuffed him. "And if I choose to walk alone and invite *attention,* as you call it, that, too, is none of your affair."

"Unless I decide to accept the invitation." His voice was harsh; he came closer.

"What do you mean?"

He reached for her, gripping her shoulders hard. She tried to pull away, but he held her, pulling her closer. "Yes, I believe I *will* accept your invitation," he said hoarsely. . . .

ELENI CARR

says she is related to "many remarkable people but no famous ones." This frequent traveler has enjoyed sojourns in both Europe and the Orient and has found that writing about these places has added extra spice to her adventures.

Dear Reader:

I'd like to take this opportunity to thank you for all your support and encouragement of Silhouette Romances.

Many of you write in regularly, telling us what you like best about Silhouette, which authors are your favorites. This is a tremendous help to us as we strive to publish the best contemporary romances possible.

All the romances from Silhouette Books are for you, so enjoy this book and the many stories to come. I hope you'll continue to share your thoughts with us, and invite you to write to us at the address below:

Karen Solem
Editor-in-Chief
Silhouette Books
P.O. Box 769
New York, N.Y. 10019

ELENI CARR
Moonlight and Memories

Silhouette Romance

Published by Silhouette Books New York

America's Publisher of Contemporary Romance

Other Silhouette Books by Eleni Carr

Mayan Moon

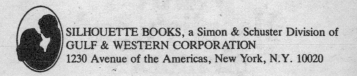

SILHOUETTE BOOKS, a Simon & Schuster Division of
GULF & WESTERN CORPORATION
1230 Avenue of the Americas, New York, N.Y. 10020

ISBN: 0-671-57168-0

First Silhouette Books printing August, 1982

10 9 8 7 6 5 4 3 2 1

Map by Tony Ferrara

America's Publisher of Contemporary Romance

Printed in the U.S.A.

Moonlight and Memories

Chapter One

As she waited in Grand Central Station for the train to South Elmsford, Helen Stathos felt different than she had that June morning. She was exhausted and crestfallen, quite a contrast to the optimistic and elated young woman who had arrived on the 9:00 A.M. train. She was furious that one man, Dr. Demetrios Criades, had been able to have this effect on her.

She had been so exuberant that morning. Just walking through the busy New York streets had been exciting, a symbol of the new life she was contemplating. She had been on her way to an interview for a position as an English teacher at the American High School in Athens.

As she had walked the eight blocks from the station to the offices of Educators International on Fiftieth Street, she had enjoyed being part of the swarm of people on Fifth Avenue. The women especially impressed Helen. They seemed so purposeful, dramatically dressed and sophisticated. She wondered if she looked like a country girl in comparison.

Helen needn't have been concerned. Her simple shirtwaist dress fit her tall, lissome figure beautifully. Its coral color suited her own eager, bright look. She looked younger than her twenty-six years. Her black hair, pulled back from her high forehead, was fastened simply at the neckline. She wore little makeup to cloud her classic features, dominated by her large, wide-set brown eyes.

Her mood had persisted while she waited in the offices of Educators International with several other candidates. She had her first inkling of danger when a woman who had just been interviewed emerged and warned the others, "Watch out for the Greek psychologist. He's as deadly as he is handsome."

She had been the last candidate to be called. Three men were sitting at a large table facing the door. They stood as she entered the room. The oldest, a ruddy, portly man with unruly white hair, reached out and shook her hand. "Nice to meet you, Miss . . ." he looked down at the folder on the table, ". . . Miss Stathos. Please sit down." He gestured to the chair facing them. "I'm Dr. Brady, principal of the American School."

So he was not the one to be feared. She looked at the other two men. The one seated next to Dr. Brady was about forty, sandy haired, with a tired but benevolent expression. He hardly fit the description of "as deadly as he is handsome." She looked at the remaining interviewer. He was younger, in his thirties, but it would be hard to guess his exact age. He had strong features, olive-toned skin and piercing dark eyes, his most compelling feature. His wiry black hair was the kind that resisted being tamed by combing.

"Stathos," he said inquiringly. "Are you Greek?"

"No . . . yes . . . that is . . ." She became confused. His look was disturbing. "You see, my grandfather was Greek, my paternal grandfather. I guess you could say I'm one-fourth Greek."

"Are you ashamed of it?" He sounded accusing.

"Of course not," she protested hotly. Why was he so antagonistic?

"My dear," Dr. Brady explained, "Dr. Criades is, as you can see, an intense nationalist. He is the consulting psychologist for our school. Since he was in New York for a professional conference we prevailed upon him to help us with the selection of staff. We have had a few problems with some of our last appointments. And this," indicating the sandy-haired man next to him, "is Jess Leigh, chairman of the Humanities Division. His wife, Allison, is also an English teacher at the school."

Jess Leigh smiled encouragingly at Helen. "Don't mind Demetrios," he said. "We've had a long day interviewing and Demetrios wasn't impressed by the other candidates. They didn't have the right feeling for Greece and its people."

"They were trying to get away from something they didn't like rather than go to something they wanted," Dr. Criades explained.

Helen was dismayed. Did that not apply to her as well? After all, she was twenty-six, educated, capable, free of family obligations now that her parents were both gone, and bored, very bored, with South Elmsford. She had been born there, gone to high school there, even commuted to a nearby college, and then had gotten a job teaching at her old high school. Except for a European trip with her parents as a child and one summer at Cape Cod while she was in college she had known no other life. Certainly she wanted to leave, but she could have chosen other destinations.

Demetrios Criades was authoritative as he continued. "One teaches not in a vacuum, but in a total environment. The environment of the American School consists of Athens and Greece as a whole, and this environment is inhabited by the Greek people. One cannot divorce that from the teaching. Don't you agree, Miss Stathos? His voice, slightly accented, was forceful.

"I don't know," she answered honestly. "I've only taught in South Elmsford. There the environment was just part of my life, familiar. But I do know that you don't just teach a subject, you teach people. My students are important. Each one is different, even in South Elmsford. I look forward to teaching young people from a different culture. I believe I would learn from them, as they would from me." Dr. Brady and Mr. Leigh nodded slightly, pleased with her answer, but Dr. Criades persisted.

"Do you really think you can adjust? After the close and familiar air of your home town? The air in Greece is very different, I think, even for one who is one-fourth Greek." His tone was sarcastic, but Helen refused to be baited.

"I'm aware of that, Dr. Criades. I don't expect Athens to be like my home town. I wouldn't want it to be. One of the reasons I'm applying for this assignment is because I remember how moved I was by a brief visit many years ago." Greece had been a special place to her from the time she was twelve. She tried to describe to the three men that summer when she had been taken on a European tour by her parents. Their stop-over in Greece had been just that, a brief stop-over in the capital for two days. Helen's mother, exhausted from traveling, had decided to rest at their hotel while Helen and her father went sight-seeing. The Acropolis had been their first stop.

She still remembered the awe with which they had climbed up to the Parthenon, its pillars stark and radiant in the sun's glare. Her father had grasped her hand so tightly that it hurt. When she had turned to look at him his eyes had shone with tears which would have fallen if he had tried to speak. That night, in their hotel room, he had read to her from Homer and fostered in her the love of Greek literature and mythology which became her passion. She had even made it her specialty in her comparative literature major at college. From that time on, Greece had had a special attraction for her. She never talked about it now that her parents were dead, though. It was too personal. She was afraid of sounding foolishly romantic, she who was thought of as such a capable and practical girl.

Yet now, in this office in New York, her voice deepened with feeling; she found herself describing that magical afternoon on the Acropolis so many years before. Although she faced Dr. Brady and Mr. Leigh as she spoke, she knew she was really addressing Demetrios Criades. When she finished, she dared to look at him, fearful that she would see a sarcastic smile or that he would make a comment ridiculing her sentiment. He said nothing. His face showed nothing.

The remainder of the interview concerned her background and experience. She felt that both the principal and the chairman were satisfied with her qualifications.

"Experience teaching each grade level of high school, a masters in European Literature, and experience running a school paper," Dr. Brady ticked off.

"Some of the others had more experience; one had a Ph.D., and the last had run the drama society, choral and dance groups at her school," Dr. Criades countered.

"For Pete's sake, Demetrios," said Jess Leigh with exasperation. "What are you looking for?"

"Someone who is honest about what she expects and what she is prepared to give," he answered coldly.

"I think I have been honest." Helen now looked at him directly. "I'm prepared to give my time, my effort, my expertise as a teacher, and my concern as a person. I also want to gain something from the experience." Her voice became spirited. "I welcome the change from a life I no longer find satisfying. I look forward to meeting new people, finding out more about a culture I already love, and finding out more about myself, as well."

"Hear, hear!" Dr. Brady said heartily. "We need keep you no longer, my dear. You've told us all we need to know. Thank you for coming in; you'll hear from us soon."

She shook hands with Dr. Brady and Mr. Leigh in turn. Then, reluctantly, she extended her hand to Demetrios Criades, intending to pull it quickly back. She couldn't; he held her hand too firmly for that. She felt suffused by warmth and her hand burned. He was forcing her to look at him. When her eyes met his she felt a force emanate from him, connecting her to him. After what seemed an eternity he released her, but said nothing. Flustered, she murmured goodbye and left.

As she had planned, she spent the afternoon shopping, but found she could not concentrate. A forbidding profile, flashing dark eyes, and the pressure of a hand clasping hers kept intruding on her thoughts, as they did now that she was back in Grand Central Station.

She had hoped to return home this afternoon feeling triumphant. Instead, she was exhausted and confused. She boarded her train and put her shopping bag on the empty seat beside her. She couldn't even remember what she had bought. Except for the bikini! Now why had she bought that scanty, bright yellow bikini? She'd never wear it. Certainly not in South Elmsford! Resolutely, she forced herself to concentrate on the travel magazine she had picked up at the newsstand.

In school the next day she tried to put the whole experience out of her mind, to busy herself with the many end-of-the-year school chores and plans. Then her cousin Andrew, who also taught at the high school, brought it up when they met for lunch. He was the only one Helen had told about the interview. Trying not to sound too disappointed, she told him she was sure she hadn't gotten the job.

Andy was surprised. "I can't imagine any administrator in his right mind turning you down."

"It wasn't the administrator who was the problem. He seemed very friendly. It was a conceited, belligerent Greek." Helen went on to describe the interview.

When she finished, Andy commented, "You may be more pessimistic than you should be. You obviously struck some kind of spark in this Dr. Criades, but the current may be one that attracts."

Helen thought about Andy's remark when she got home that afternoon. No way, she decided. Being rude was hardly a sign of being attracted to someone. She was probably well rid of any venture which would involve exposure to the dangerous Dr. Criades.

But what will I do this summer? she wondered. Just then the telephone rang.

It was Jess Leigh. "Dr. Brady and I have been trying to call you all day. He's leaving tonight and I'm booked on a flight to Athens tomorrow. I'm glad I finally got you. Putting it all in a letter isn't as satisfactory."

Her heart sank. "I was at school all day. I appreciate your getting in touch with me personally this way. To . . . to let me down easy, I guess."

"Let you down?" He sounded surprised. "What do you mean? Unless signing a contract to spend the next two years teaching with us at the American School is a let-down? Did you change your mind?"

"Change my mind? Oh, no . . . I mean . . . of course I want . . . more than ever . . ." She tried to collect herself. "I just wasn't very optimistic after the interview.

"Why on earth not? You made quite an impression."

"You and Dr. Brady were very gracious, but Dr. Criades made his disapproval obvious."

"You're wrong, Miss Stathos," Jess assured her. "The decision to offer you the position was unanimous."

"Then you must have used all your powers of persuasion to get him to agree."

"Not a bit," he insisted. "You just don't know Demetrios. He sometimes seems harsh; he tends to ask very probing questions. On the other hand, he can also be friendly, helpful, and quite gentle. He's also a great judge of people and he supported your candidacy."

Jess Leigh sounded sincere, but Helen was unconvinced. He was probably being diplomatic, she thought. "I find that hard to believe, Mr. Leigh. But perhaps we'll both change our first impressions when we work together in Athens."

What had happened to her conviction that she wanted no part of any venture which included contact with Demetrios Criades?

"Yes, I'm sure you'll feel differently when you get to know Demetrios—*if* you have a chance to get to know him better, that is. He's not at the school full time, you know. Only on a consulting basis. He may not be around that much."

"Oh . . ." Helen should have been relieved. Why did she feel disappointment instead? "I just thought . . . You seem to know him so well that I assumed . . ." She broke off.

"We are friends outside of school. Allison and I are both very fond of Demetrios. He's quite a guy when you get to know him. We're all pretty friendly at the American School, Helen. Ours is a small, close-knit faculty and we don't stand on ceremony."

"I appreciate that, Mr. Leigh."

"Call me Jess, please. When do you think you can be ready to leave, Helen?"

"Ready? Why, I don't know. Is there any urgency? Do you have something you want me to work on this summer, like a curriculum committee?" Helen was confused.

"Of course not." Jess laughed. "I just think it's a good idea for you to spend the summer getting acquainted with Greece and Athens . . . and all of us. After all, it's going to be your home for the next two years, perhaps longer, if you get to love it as Allison and I do. It may be a small country, but there's no end to its beauties. I can't wait to get back."

"Are all three of you returning tomorrow?" Helen made her voice casual.

"No. As I said, Dr. Brady is off tonight and Demetrios apparently doesn't like airplanes. Look, I'd better sign off because I'm building up quite a phone bill. The contract will be in the mail tomorrow, along with all the instructions about travel arrangements and expenses, housing, the school calendar and a million other things. If you have any questions call Educators International and they'll be glad to help. But take my advice and come over soon. Allison and I will be glad to help you get settled. I really look forward to working with you, Helen."

"I do too, Jess. Thank you so much for calling personally. Have a good trip home."

"Right. Hope to see you soon." He rang off.

Helen could hardly believe it was really going to happen. She was apprehensive, but elated. They really wanted her. But did "they" really include Demetrios Criades?

She decided to take Jess's advice and make her travel arrangements immediately. Summer in

Greece! How exciting that sounded. She could be there within a week.

Then again, she thought, she had never been on a cruise. A week or more at sea would give her time to relax and get her thoughts together.

Yes, she decided, she would definitely go by ship, if she could get passage. It should be possible, she thought. Most people today, like Dr. Brady and Jess, traveled by air. Except those who didn't like airplanes.

That night, a dark face intruded into her dreams.

The next ten days were hectic. She had managed to get passage on the Olympia, leaving for Athens from New York on July eleventh. That gave her so little time to get everything done. After submitting her resignation she had to deal with last-minute shopping, packing, closing the apartment, making banking arrangements and goodbyes, all of which left her feeling both sad and exhilarated. She was also completely exhausted.

The morning of her departure dawned brightly. Having slept but little in her excitement, Helen was at her bedroom window when the sun rose. South Elmsford had never looked lovelier than on that clear summer morning. She looked down at the quiet street lined with green lawns, clipped hedges and neat white fences. It looked so peaceful—and so permanent. She felt a qualm about leaving. Was she doing the right thing? The image of dark, brooding eyes in a stern, chiseled face flashed before her. Resolutely, she put the doubts out of her mind. She was committed.

Despite her insistence that she wanted to leave without fanfare, Andy had insisted on accompanying

her to New York. "You can't just slink off," he had
decided. "A little Bon Voyage party is in order.
Besides, I've never been on board an ocean liner;
you can't spoil my fun."

At the pier the crowds, the confusion and the
noise were overwhelming. Andy succeeded in steer-
ing her into the large passengers' lounge on the A
deck, where farewell festivities were well under way
already. Despite the crowds, he was even able to
commandeer a table. He set down their picnic
hamper triumphantly.

"Now for the champagne and caviar and a proper
Bon Voyage."

Helen smiled at his exuberance. "You look more
like the happy departing passenger than I do," she
noted. "Postpone the cork popping for ten minutes
while I find my cabin, deposit my things and freshen
up."

A steward showed Helen to her cabin and opened
the door. A young woman was combing her hair,
looking into the mirror above the dressing table.
Since Helen had booked for a double cabin to save
money, she was unsurprised.

"Hello," the other woman said. "I'm Lisa
Rhodes, your roommate. The travel agent told me
your name, but I'm afraid I've forgotten it."

Lisa Rhodes was about Helen's age, or perhaps a
year or two older, and quite striking. Her blond hair,
short and feathery, framed a tanned face, blue eyes,
and a sensuously shaped mouth. Her small, curva-
ceous figure was emphasized by the clinging wrap-
around jersey dress she wore.

"My name is Stathos, Helen Stathos."

The other girl surveyed her coolly. "First trip?"
she asked.

"First ocean trip," Helen admitted. "I'm really looking forward to it."

"Oh, the crossing should be fun." Lisa glanced at Helen's left hand. "Not married?"

Helen shook her head.

"Neither am I," Lisa announced with satisfaction. "Not anymore. In fact, I'm celebrating my new state of single blessedness, thanks to the Mexican divorce court's fast service. So now it's back home to Greece for me. And I intend to keep celebrating all the way across the Atlantic."

Helen didn't know what to say. Did divorce call for a celebration? Not in South Elmsford. She smiled weakly.

Lisa continued blithely. "I've already met a young officer who looks promising. I'm sure he has a friend. Well, see you later. I've got to join my parents and friends on deck and pretend to be sorry I'm leaving." With a grin and a little wave, she departed.

Alone, Helen hung her jacket in the small closet and took her turn at the mirror. How tired she looked! She carefully started to freshen up. Just scrubbing her face and splashing it with cold water made her feel better. She used very little makeup, but took pains with it, even so.

Why was she so concerned about looking attractive? Certainly not for her cousin. What about the arrogant young psychologist who didn't like airplanes? There weren't many departures by ship to Greece. It was perfectly possible that he, too . . . She tried to dismiss the thought.

Even if he had booked for this crossing the ship was so large that their paths might never cross. Not that she wanted to see him, anyway. Nevertheless, she took more time than usual to freshen up, reapply her lipstick and brush her hair into shining obedience.

She returned to the lounge, which seemed to have become even more crowded. She made her way through the milling, laughing people. The gaiety was becoming contagious. Lisa had said it would be a good trip and Helen, too, was determined to make it so.

When she reached Andy he complained, "Hey, about time. I'm dying for that champagne." He handed her a glass. "I'm glad to see you've revived," he said. I was getting impatient, but you're worth the wait."

Helen took the glass and grinned at him.

"In fact," Andy continued, "you look great."

"Indeed you do," said another voice, familiar, deep and suggestive. "You look quite different from our first meeting."

She felt as if she were on fire and tried to concentrate on what Andy was saying.

". . . and we got to talking and I found out that Demetrios is associated with your school in Athens. Isn't that a coincidence? He was alone, so I asked him to join us. I was sure you wouldn't mind."

Helen didn't know what to say. Forcing herself to look at Demetrios Criades, she was unnerved by his penetrating gaze. Would he always have this effect on her, making her feel so unsure? Andy rescued her from needing to reply.

"I think it's just great that you two are at the same school," he said to Demetrios. "Helen is alone in the world, you know. I hope you'll keep an eye on her in Athens."

Helen was indignant as she declared, "I certainly

don't need a protector. I'm perfectly capable of looking out for myself. Keep your advice to yourself."

"O.K., O.K." Andy smilingly held up his hands. "My cousin can be quite a spitfire when she's angry, Demetrios. Better watch out."

"I see I shall have to be wary," Demetrios said softly. Was he making fun of her?

Andy proposed a toast. "To a happy journey, Helen. To an exciting two years and to your eventual return home."

They all raised their glasses. "I can drink to most of that," Demetrios murmured as he tipped his glass to her before drinking. Andy kept the champagne flowing. His funny toasts had them all laughing and soon Helen forgot her anger at him. Even Demetrios was laughing. He looked so different when he laughed, so relaxed. She hoped her own tension didn't show.

She attributed her inner excitement to the imminent departure and to the champagne. How many glasses had she had? She had lost count. Her head was light and giddy when she heard the call of "All ashore."

Andy stood to wish her a last farewell. Suddenly she noticed that Lisa had joined them.

"Hello, again," Lisa greeted Helen. "My group of well-wishers left already, fortunately." She paused. "I see you're still saying goodbye to your friends."

Helen introduced Lisa, who looked at the two men appraisingly.

The "All Ashore" was sounded again.

"If you don't go you'll find yourself on an ocean voyage," Helen cautioned.

"Nothing wrong with that except I don't have a

toothbrush. So I guess we'll have to go ashore." Andy kissed his cousin fondly.

"I feel left out." Lisa pouted and turned to Demetrios. "Mind if I bid you a fond farewell?" Without waiting for an answer, she reached up archly and planted a kiss on his lips.

He didn't resist, simply smiled and told her, "I'm traveling with you, but thank you anyway."

"So much the better," Lisa declared. "Hello kisses are more promising than goodbye ones, don't you think?"

"Well, if that's the case, and to get into the spirit . . ." Before Helen realized what was happening she found herself roughly pulled into Demetrios's arms. When she tried to draw away, his arms tightened. His face came closer and she could see the amber flecks in his dark eyes. She felt dizzy, unable to protest. "Consider this a hello," he whispered. Then his mouth closed on hers and the world disappeared.

All her resistance faded as her body molded itself to his. His kiss became more passionate and searching and she couldn't keep from responding in kind. When Demetrios finally ended the kiss Helen realized that she would never have had the willpower to do so herself.

Demetrios kept his arms lightly about her to support her as he murmured, "Lisa is right. Hello kisses are much more promising, don't you think?"

Chapter Two

Helen stood at the rail with Lisa as the ship pulled slowly away from the dock. She felt spent.

"Well, that's that," Lisa said briskly. "Enough of farewells. Let's get ready for the pleasures of the trip. And . . ." she drawled speculatively, "I hope one of them will be the intriguing Dr. Criades. Where did you say you had met him?"

After Helen explained about the interview Lisa exclaimed with envy, "You mean you'll be working together? Lucky you!"

"Not really working together. He's a consultant, not at the school all the time. I don't expect I'll see that much of him." To herself she added, Which will suit me just fine. Then, curiously, Helen asked, "How come you're going back to Greece . . . I mean, after the divorce and all?"

"I still have the apartment," Lisa explained. "Jeff, my former husband, is with the foreign service and he's been reassigned."

"I'm sorry," Helen said. "I mean, about the divorce."

"Oh, don't be," Lisa protested.

"What are you going to do now?"

"I'm not sure. I may just sell everything and wind up my affairs in Athens. On the other hand," she continued with a speculative smile, "I may not. With Demetrios Criades there, Athens may hold a new attraction."

"You know, Lisa, he could be married," Helen said. She hadn't allowed herself to think of this possibility before.

"No way. Greeks usually wear wedding bands and I made sure to look right away. He wasn't. And judging by the way he relished those hello embraces he's not averse to romance."

Helen flushed.

"And neither am I," Lisa continued. "You shouldn't be, either. We're both young, free—a new feeling for me—over twenty-one and reasonably attractive. It should be a great trip." She spread her hands expansively. "We'll soon be in international waters, conducive to a more liberal view of, shall we say, international relations. And speaking of international relations, here's a prospect who looks eager for closer ties." A young ship's officer was approaching them.

"Ahoy, Hercules," Lisa greeted him. "We've embarked. You must promise to take good care of us on the high seas. This is Helen's first voyage, but I, too, shall need constant attention."

The young man smiled, his teeth very white against the deep bronze of his face. His English was fluent, but accented as he answered. "It will be a source of unending pleasure for me to care for you and your beautiful companion." His blue eyes were riveted on Helen. "Ten days of such duty will be paradise."

"Hercules Phyllos, let me introduce you to Helen Stathos." Lisa turned to Helen and warned, "Watch out for these blond, blue-eyed Greek men. They must have some northern European blood that gives them their good looks and glib tongues. Most Greek men are dark and silent. Mind you," she chided, touching Hercules's cheek, "I'm not complaining. I like the contrast. Not that my preference is going to do me much good now that you've met Helen. Well, you'll just have to find me a replacement. After all, I did meet you first."

Hercules smiled broadly, obviously enjoying the flattery. He really was handsome, Helen thought, rather like a statue of Hermes she had once seen in a museum.

As if she had read Helen's thoughts, Lisa proposed, "Just find me another young Greek god." She paused, her eyes attracted to someone approaching. It was Demetrios Criades. "Although perhaps you won't have to," she told Hercules, then turned her attention to the newcomer. "I was hoping we'd see you." She introduced the two men. They sized each other up as Lisa continued gayly, "Why don't we arrange to be at the same table for dinner? We'll have to sign up right away to get the second sitting, won't we, Hercules?"

"That is the preferred sitting," Hercules agreed. "Older people and family groups tend to take the first sitting. I myself will be dining at the second sitting."

Demetrios noticed that this was said directly to Helen and smiled sardonically.

Helen noticed the smile. "It doesn't really matter, does it?" she asked.

"It makes no difference to me," Demetrios said.

Hercules was gallant. "I shall arrange for both the young ladies to sit with me at the captain's table." To Demetrios he added unconvincingly, "You, also, of course, Dr. Criades."

"No need to go out of your way." Demetrios's tone was cool. "It's of no consequence."

Helen felt a strange emptiness. She looked down at her hands. So he did not care to be with her . . . with them, she corrected herself.

"But it is to me," Lisa persisted. "Herc, do try. Remember, you owe me a replacement."

Hercules looked from her to Demetrios, then to Helen, who had hardly glanced at the psychologist. Apparently satisfied that Demetrios was no rival for the girl he himself favored, he said to Lisa, "I believe I can arrange it."

"Fantastic," Lisa gloated. "We'll all have a ball together."

Helen wasn't so sure.

"How about an ouzo in the lounge?" Lisa suggested. "They should be serving by now. We'll celebrate the start of our voyage and initiate Helen into some pleasant Greek customs."

"I should so much like to initiate Helen into our way of life. I am at your service." Hercules bowed slightly as he addressed Helen.

"*Tourists* need guides. Miss Stathos . . . Helen . . . is not coming as a tourist," Demetrios said coolly to Hercules. "Or are you?" he asked Helen.

"No, of course not. I'll be working." She stopped as she noticed the young officer's hurt expression.

"But it will all be new to me and I would appreciate the services of a guide."

Hercules smiled.

"The guide may sometimes come between the viewer and the experience," Demetrios said without expression. "Useful if one needs an interpreter for life, but no substitute for actual experience."

"Let's continue this philosophical discussion in the lounge, although I'd prefer a lighter topic. Come on," Lisa urged.

Helen tried to excuse herself. "I think I'll beg off. I'd rather rest before dinner."

"But you have hours before dinner." Hercules took her arm. "And I have only one hour before I go on duty. You cannot abandon me now. We have much to learn of each other." He was earnest and charming and not to be denied. Demetrios said nothing. Helen gave in and soon found herself seated next to Hercules in the lounge.

She really was tired and found it hard to concentrate on the increasingly ardent talk of the handsome ship's officer. Her head was swimming. She declined a drink but Hercules insisted she try the Greek liqueur which the waiter brought in a decanter.

The ouzo looked innocent enough as Demetrios poured the clear liquid into each glass. "But mine is only half-full," Helen pointed out.

"It's a strong drink, our ouzo. You're tired. Combined with the champagne it may be too potent a combination. After all, your cousin asked me to look out for you," Demetrios said quietly.

"As I said before, I don't need looking after." Helen was furious. "Fill my glass and let me worry about potent combinations."

Demetrios did as requested, commenting as he did so, "Ah, the spitfire emerges again." He looked directly at her as he raised his glass. *"Yassou!"* he toasted.

She took a sip. It had a pleasant, licorice taste. Feeling his eyes still on her, she took a deeper draught and felt herself suffused in a rosy warmth. He was right. It was indeed potent. She didn't want him to see the effect the ouzo was having and was grateful when Lisa distracted him.

Helen finished her drink slowly. She was finding it difficult to follow the story Hercules was relating.

"So, you see, I have a good career ahead of me," he was saying. "I expect to captain my own ship soon. I am ambitious, not like the other officers who care only to amuse themselves with the tourists. Not that I mind some fun," his glance flicked over to Lisa, "but I wish to find a serious young woman with whom I can have a more permanent relationship." He gazed at Helen with admiration; there was no mistaking his meaning.

She was flattered, but had difficulty focusing on his face. She looked away, trying to clear her head, and encountered Demetrios's eyes. He looked both amused and disapproving.

Suddenly very uncomfortable, Helen stood up. "I really am exhausted," she said apologetically to Hercules.

He was immediately contrite. "Of course, I have been selfish. It is almost time for me to report. I shall escort you to your stateroom."

"The potent combination?" Demetrios was sarcastic.

She turned and walked away without replying.

Feeling shaky, she was grateful for the support of Hercules's arm as they walked out.

"I'll be down in a while," Lisa called. Demetrios said nothing more, but she felt him staring into her back.

Back at her stateroom, she had difficulty unlocking the door. Hercules took the key from her shaky hand, opened the door and followed her in. Inside, he put his hands on her shoulders. Helen panicked as she saw his face draw close.

"No, don't! What are you . . . ?"

"Don't worry. I'm in no hurry," he said softly. "We have the whole voyage to get to know each other." He bent and kissed her lightly on the lips. "I'll pick you up for dinner."

After he left Helen closed the door and leaned back against it. She was sorry she had discouraged his kiss. If she had not, perhaps the memory of that earlier kiss from Demetrios would not be so troubling. She was so tired. She pushed herself away from the door and lay down on the bed.

As soon as she closed her eyes she began to relive the passionate response Demetrios had commanded. The world splintered behind her eyelids and its colors eddied in dizzying shapes. She would feel different when the effects had faded, when she had rested. She drifted into sleep.

When she awoke two hours later she realized that Lisa must have come in to change while she had been sleeping. Lisa's dress, the one she had worn that afternoon, was carelessly thrown across her bed.

She's probably hoping I'll sleep through dinner, Helen thought grumpily. That way Lisa would have both men to herself. Well, Helen decided, she certainly wasn't going to give her roommate that satisfaction.

After she showered she felt much better. She dressed with care. The dress she selected, a honey beige with a straight skirt, provocatively slit in front, was very becoming. It was sleeveless, with a wide, square neckline which showed off her shoulders and delicate throat.

She brushed a bright coral lipstick on her lips, then looked into the mirror with approval. Helen wet her lips with her tongue, then tried to dismiss the memory that the touch on her lips evoked. Even so, she felt herself flushing when she heard Hercules knock.

"Are you ready?" he asked, smiling at her, when she opened the door. He looked at her with undisguised admiration. "You look ready for anything."

But was she? She wasn't sure when she saw Demetrios and Lisa at their table in the large and impressive dining room. Demetrios greeted Hercules curtly, then asked her, "Are you feeling better?"

"Yes, of course." She, too, was curt. "I'm fine. Please don't trouble yourself." She saw a dark expression come over his face and immediately was sorry. Perhaps he had meant to be solicitous, not sarcastic as she had assumed. No matter what attitude she took with this enigmatic man it seemed to be wrong. Well, she wouldn't let it bother her. She meant to enjoy herself this evening.

Dining at the captain's table proved to be delightful. Captain Demos was charming. He delivered a gracious toast to the assemblage.

"I wish to welcome you all aboard the Olympia. We look forward to a good crossing. Here is to good weather, good fellowship, good times. And for tonight, a good appetite. It is our pleasure to have you all aboard."

As he sat down to hearty applause, Captain Demos raised his glass again to Helen, who was seated next to him. "It is especially a pleasure to have *you* aboard, young lady. I am fortunate to have such a lovely girl seated next to me. I commend Hercules and appreciate his allowing me to share your attention."

The distinguished, white-haired captain had an old-world charm, Helen decided. Perhaps Hercules, too, would develop it with time, replacing the present boyish enthusiasm he displayed. She enjoyed talking to the captain and was disappointed when he excused himself before dessert arrived.

"You should be flattered," Hercules remarked after his departure. "He almost never stays this long."

When Helen looked surprised he explained. "The captain dines early and very simply in his cabin. He joins us for a little while at dinner as a social gesture. It is expected. But I cannot say that I am disappointed at his departure." He took her hand. "I do not like anyone taking your attention from me." Basking in his admiration, Helen left her hand in his. It was nice to feel vivacious and desirable.

Why not? she thought. Here she was on her first night at sea being courted by a dashing young officer. It was romantic and uncomplicated, not like the confused emotions Demetrios Criades aroused in her.

Demetrios and Lisa sat on the other side of Hercules. Helen thought this a fortunate circumstance, since it kept her from direct contact with the piercing eyes of the young psychologist. Still, she knew she was conscious of his presence, and caught herself trying to catch snatches of his conversation with Lisa.

The others at the table were a congenial group: two middle-aged men, both on the faculty of a southern university, and a distinguished elderly couple, the Graysons, antique dealers from San Francisco.

The professors were describing the excavations on the island of Santorini, which was their ultimate destination in Greece. Apparently they had caught Demetrios's interest.

"What an interesting undertaking," Helen heard him remark.

"If one enjoys digging among the rocks in a dusty ruin," Hercules whispered to Helen. "You and I, I think, will have more pleasurable things to do."

Another voice intruded abruptly. "Would you pour me some coffee, Helen? The carafe is there by you." Demetrios was leaning over, holding out his cup. "That is, if you can disengage yourself for a moment." He looked down coldly at her hand.

She realized that her hand was still held tightly in Hercules's. What did Demetrios think? She needn't care what he thought, she told herself. After all, she was free to do as she wished. He was the last person whose opinion should concern her.

Demetrios stood up. "But then, I needn't bother you," he said as he walked over and took the seat next to her, the chair the captain had vacated. Demetrios poured his coffee but, to Hercules's annoyance, did not resume his own place.

Helen tried to concentrate on what Hercules was saying. Apparently he wanted her to know everything about him, almost as if he were offering his credentials.

"And so, you see, Helen, I spend much of my time with English-speaking people. My mother and sister also speak English well, as you will see. We know very much about American customs. I have even become quite proficient at dancing as you do in the States. There will be disco music in the cabaret tonight. You shall judge if I am as good as your American boyfriends."

"No American boyfriends, Hercules," Helen protested.

"So much the better for me," Hercules said with satisfaction. "No competition. I have been hoping to meet someone like you on one of my voyages."

He looked so sincere that Helen told herself that this was what she wanted, too. She needed something ego-boosting and romantic to help her start her new life.

"Listen, you two." It was Lisa interrupting. "Why don't we catch the show in the cabaret and do a little dancing?"

"Yes, let us go down," Hercules seconded her. "But I shall have to leave you at twelve to go on duty again." He turned to Helen. "Is that all right?"

They rose and Helen took his arm. "Of course it's all right." She smiled vivaciously at Hercules. "Perhaps I'll be lucky and they'll play some slow, romantic music so I can rest." She knew such flirtatious comments were not like her. Was she acting like this for Hercules's benefit? He obviously approved. Or for Demetrios's?

The nightclub was noisy, crowded and garish. There was no larger table available, so they were forced to crowd around a table for two near the dance floor. The four of them were so crowded together around the small table that Helen could not keep from touching Demetrios in some way. Whenever her shoulder or arm touched his she pulled away as if burned. She felt his knee against hers, but she couldn't move her legs without stepping on Hercules. Her cheeks were burning, and not because of the heat in the cabaret. When Hercules asked her to dance she rose gratefully and they moved out to the floor.

"You're really very good. It must take hours of practicing with all the young ladies on your cruises," she teased after a few minutes.

"Ah, but never before with so lovely a partner as you. See how all the men watch with envy?"

They danced several dances and then returned, out of breath, to the table.

"Don't you dance, Dr. Criades?" Hercules asked.

"Not these new dances, I'm afraid," Demetrios answered.

"But you spent four years studying in the States," Lisa pointed out. "Didn't they dance at the University of Massachusetts?"

"Oh, *they* did, but *I* could not." He emphasized the pronouns. "I was too busy studying and working to support myself."

So that was how he had learned English so well, Helen thought. She tried to picture him as a lonely young student with no time for fun. He had never had the opportunity to be young and carefree.

There was a brief fanfare and then the Master of Ceremonies announced, "And now, for our more romantic patrons, a medley of old favorites." The band launched into a slow and dreamy tune.

"Well, here's one you can certainly do." Lisa pulled Demetrios onto the dance floor.

Helen watched them. They moved well together, Lisa dancing closely in unison with Demetrios. Hercules reminded Helen that he would have to go on duty shortly and asked her to dance again.

The floor had become so crowded that they could hardly move. They had to dance in place, rocking rhythmically.

"I think I like this," Hercules said, grinning. "I can hold you so close in public and pretend to dance and it is all right and proper."

She should scold him, she thought, but found it was restful just to relax like this for the next several dances. She soon felt a growing tension in Hercules, however, and was relieved when the slow music ended. Hercules reluctantly released her. As she stepped back she bumped into Lisa.

They had started to walk back to the table when the disco beat started again. "Helen, you don't mind, do you?" Lisa begged. "Just a temporary change of partners?" She grabbed Hercules's arm and started dancing in place. Helplessly, he shrugged at Helen as if to say, "What can I do?" and let himself be led away.

Demetrios said nothing. He stood quietly as the dancers whirled around them. Helen was embarrassed. "Are we just going to stand here getting trampled on?" she asked nervously.

Still without speaking, he took her elbow firmly and steered her through the dancers and the maze of tables to the outside deck.

The air was refreshing after the closeness inside. It felt cool and salty. Helen drew a deep breath as she leaned on the rail. "I guess I did need some fresh air after the noise and smoke and crowds."

"Yes," he agreed softly. "Often the mind is more clouded by emotions and choices than by smoke and noise. That's why I brought you outside."

"You've been watching me," she accused.

Darkness hid his expression as he replied. "I have, as you well know. You're like a flower, expectant and open. The bees will flock."

She flushed with anger. "That's insulting. I am certainly not 'expectant' of anything. There are no bees . . . or perhaps only one." She became confused. "He's just an acquaintance, just a boy." She was overreacting. She didn't have to explain herself to him.

"Hardly a boy," Demetrios disagreed. "Hercules is a young man with very serious intentions. And even if you deny being 'expectant' you can hardly deny that you're certainly raising his expectations. That dancing was nothing but an excuse for an intimate embrace. You're raising his hopes by playing up to him in public."

"Playing up to him!" She was indignant. "I'm not playing up to him," she lied.

"Well, if that's the way you dance in America I wasted my four years there. Perhaps you'll help me make up for lost time. Teach me to dance your way." He pulled her close, and it took all her strength to wrench away as she felt herself weakening. She clasped the rail behind her for support and tried to catch her breath.

Darkness masked his expression, but she heard him draw in his breath heavily and quickly. She gasped as he came toward her, but he only took her chin in his hand and raised her face. She couldn't keep from looking into the grim face which emerged from the shadows.

"Your cousin said you lacked experience, but I'm not sure he's right. If you decided to come to Greece to find a husband or to have an affair, you're acting suitably."

"Take me back inside. I don't want to listen to any more of your analyses, Dr. Criades." She couldn't keep her voice from trembling slightly.

He gazed at her deeply for a moment, then dropped his hand.

As they stepped back inside she turned to him with an angry warning. "And I'll thank you to stop watching me and to stay out of my affairs."

"Your 'affairs' may be too much for you to handle," he said, raising one dark brow.

She instantly regretted her choice of words. He was infuriating, but before she could think of a proper retort, Hercules appeared.

"There you are. I have been looking for you."

"It was warm in here; we went outside for some air," Demetrios said smoothly as they returned to the table where Lisa was waiting, looking impatient.

"Where were you?" she asked. "The show's about to start."

Hercules looked at his watch. "The show already? I am late." He did not appear too chagrined as he continued. "Helen, you have made me lose all track of time. Will you stay for the performance or shall I walk you to your room?"

"You don't want to be later than you already are," Helen answered. "You go on. I'm perfectly capable of seeing myself back to my cabin."

"I'll escort both ladies to their stateroom after we see the performance," Demetrios said, oblivious to Lisa's look of protest.

Hercules took Helen's hand and brought it to his lips. "I shall see you at lunch tomorrow. My afternoon will be free; we can spend it together." His tone was possessive. He quickly said good night and left.

"He takes a lot for granted, doesn't he?" Demetrios whispered.

Helen didn't reply; she was grateful that the show started promptly. It was the usual kind of variety show: a comedian, a singer, exhibition dancers and a magician. She had become engrossed in her own thoughts when the last act was announced, a series of Greek folk dances. They were performed by a group of young men she recognized as members of the crew.

"Look," Helen commented. "The sailors are dancing. Is this part of their job?"

"Not quite." Demetrios smiled. "They do it for the fun of it. Most of these young men are from the islands. Dancing has always been part of their lives."

"There are no officers dancing," Helen observed.

Demetrios's smile stiffened. "The officers are usually city men, like your Lt. Phyllos who, I am sure, prefers American dances."

"He's not my . . ." Helen started to protest. Then she stopped. She wasn't going to answer to him. He had again succeeded in putting her on the defensive. "I think I'll turn in," she announced abruptly as she stood up. "I'm really very tired."

"But the performance isn't over," Lisa protested. "It's not finished yet."

"I know, but I'm finished . . . beat. Lisa, you

have your key. You two stay and enjoy the rest of the show."

Without waiting for a reply, and without so much as a look at Demetrios, she walked away. When she reached the door she was irritated to see that he had followed her.

"I don't need an escort," she snapped. "I am perfectly capable of finding my way to my own room."

"I don't doubt it," was his reply, "but it is our custom, the Hellenic custom, to see a lady safely to her door. Old-fashioned, perhaps, but I am sure your young officer would approve."

"He is not *my* young officer. And *you* are not my protector."

"And *you* are not behaving like a reasonable young lady."

"That's my privilege. Now leave me alone; go back to Lisa. Perhaps her behavior suits you better."

"Perhaps it does." He turned on his heel and returned to the table.

As she walked down the narrow corridor toward her cabin, Helen knew she would not be able to sleep. Some fresh air might help.

Out on deck, the night air was refreshing as she walked toward the bow of the ship. She was vaguely aware of other passengers taking a turn on deck, or of couples talking quietly as they stood at the rail.

She stood for a long time, looking out at the darkness, listening to the rush of the water. The air was dense and still, the ocean smooth. Yet she could see nothing but a dark face with piercing eyes. Demetrios . . .

Suddenly the face in her mind materialized in the darkness before her, a grim and angry Demetrios.

"Where were you? I took Lisa to your cabin and you weren't there."

"I changed my mind; I decided to take a walk." Why was she explaining?

"One does not walk alone—in the dark. It's like an invitation. Or perhaps you were not alone?"

"That's none of your business," she said, knowing that she was fanning his anger.

"Were you with Hercules?"

"I said that it's none of your affair whether I was with someone or not. And if I choose to walk alone and invite attention, that, too, is none of your affair."

"Unless I decide to accept the invitation." His voice was harsh as he came closer.

"What do you mean?"

He reached for her, gripping her shoulders hard. She tried to pull away, but he held her, pulling her closer. "Yes, I believe I *will* accept the invitation," he said hoarsely. He strained her to him and his mouth closed on hers.

She felt panic; then, gradually, as the long kiss continued, draining her of her anger, she felt something else. Her blood raced, responding to the insistency of his demand. Her fists uncurled and she felt her hands flatten against his chest.

Demetrios felt her respond. Groaning softly against her lips, he parted them demandingly with renewed passion. For the second time that day he blotted out the world. He became the world. They moved together until she felt the full length of his body with hers.

Someone walked by, jostling Demetrios as the ship pitched a little. Startled, Demetrios pulled away.

"Sorry, old man! Oh, young lady, too. Really, so sorry . . ." Embarrassed, the dark shape hurried off.

Helen came to her senses. Her hands were still on his shoulders; her bruised mouth was still warm from his kiss.

She pushed him away and raced to her stateroom. He didn't try to stop her, but she felt him following behind until she was safely inside the door.

"Where've you been?" Lisa asked sleepily from her bed.

"Just out for a walk," Helen answered briefly. "Please, Lisa, I'm tired. I don't feel like talking. I just want to sleep."

But she knew that sleep would be long in coming that night.

Chapter Three

Helen spent a restless night. The room was hot and her mind was in turmoil. Finally, toward dawn, she fell into an exhausted, troubled sleep. She slept straight through the breakfast hour and awakened at eleven to an empty stateroom. She hadn't even heard Lisa go out.

She got out of bed and looked out through her porthole. It was a brilliant, golden morning. She didn't belong in it, she thought. It contrasted too much with the darkness in her head. Perhaps she would just spend the day in the cabin, recuperating. From what? She was being silly, she knew, but she just couldn't think yet.

There was a knock at the door. It proved to be the steward. "Miss Stathos, Dr. Criades ordered a pot of coffee for you. I took the liberty of adding some fresh rolls."

"Dr. Criades . . ." Of all the insolence! She was about to refuse, to send the tray back. Here he was interfering in her life again! But the steward was already putting the tray down and she smelled the fresh coffee. Weighing her indignation against the delicious aroma, she succumbed. She thanked the steward and, when he left, poured herself a cup gratefully.

Her head cleared. She would just sort things out, put them in proper perspective. After all, nothing shattering had occurred. She had been tired by all the activity and excitement. She had also probably been feeling the effects of the champagne and the ouzo. She had simply let herself be carried away by Demetrios's embrace. No big thing. It had no special meaning, no matter what he thought . . . if he thought about it at all.

Maybe that was how he behaved with any available woman. Both times his touch had been without affection. She tried to picture him acting differently. Could he hold her and express love, not anger? She had to stop this! She was confusing herself again. He did not and would not!

Yet he had thought of her this morning in ordering the coffee. She didn't know how to interpret his behavior. Was he being considerate or just domineering?

The phone rang and she answered. "So, you are still in your room. Good morning, sleepyhead."

It was Hercules. At least his actions weren't hard to interpret. He was all eager interest, admiration and plans. He had thought of her all night. He would see her at lunch at one-thirty. They would swim after lunch. He was free until four. He would count the minutes. He hung up.

His enthusiasm was hard to resist. Helen's natural verve was returning. Why should she spend the day in the cabin? There was so much to do. She would explore the ship before meeting Hercules for lunch. She would be as cheerful and bright as the day.

Now, what should she wear? She needed something in keeping with her jaunty, new attitude. She settled for straight leg jeans in a light blue, brushed denim, topped with a brightly printed halter top. She had some misgivings at having to wear the top without a bra, but there was no way to conceal the straps. "Everyone wears this braless," the saleslady had said. So be it! She would, too.

Since it was already warm and promised to get even more sultry, she pulled her hair back and off her neck, tying it ponytail fashion with a strip of red wool. No makeup, she decided, just a touch of crimson lipstick. She wanted to feel as scrubbed and bright as the morning.

"Voila," she said to her image in the mirror." You're ready to face the world . . . I hope."

Her first stop was at the social activities area near the dining room to pick up a ship's directory. People were gathered around a large, cork bulletin board on which were posted the day's activities. Helen looked at the offerings: films, dance instruction, concerts and lectures.

Lessons and lectures, she thought. Not for me. I'll have enough of those when I'm teaching again this fall. Although conversational Greek might be helpful. Suddenly a particular entry caught her eye and made her catch her breath.

LECTURE . . . DR. DEMETRIOS CRIADES . . . "THE GREEK TEMPERAMENT" 4 P.M.

Certainly a suitable topic for that temperamental Greek, she thought almost maliciously.

Picking up her directory, she was about to turn away when the receptionist asked, "Don't you want the Activities Bulletin? There should be some interesting possibilities for you."

Helen accepted the bulletin the woman held out to her.

Yes, some interesting possibilities. Well, she reasoned, why not go to the lecture? She was going to make Athens her home for a while. Perhaps his talk would be enlightening. And, after all, she might very well be involved with him, in a professional capacity, in the future. Personal involvement, that was what she had to avoid.

As she wandered, Helen realized that avoiding someone on the Olympia would not be difficult. There were so many public rooms, recreation areas and cubby holes that she could easily get lost and stay that way. When she stopped at the ship's library she discovered the one place she would have to avoid. There was Demetrios, sitting in an armchair, absorbed in a book. He was formally dressed, white shirt, tie and jacket, in contrast to the other passengers she had encountered, all of whom had been colorfully and casually attired.

She stood in the doorway and looked at him for a moment. The sun streaming in from the window behind his chair was sending light beams through his dark, springy hair and casting a golden glow on his strong features.

Helen wasn't ready to face him after the way they had parted last night. Just thinking about it made her cheeks burn. She was about to slip away when he raised his head.

"Come in, little girl. Are you looking for a book to read?"

Hadn't he recognized her? She became embarrassed. "No . . . that is . . . not exactly. I didn't want to interrupt. . . . It's me, Helen Stathos. I'm not exactly a little girl," she finished lamely.

He rose and walked over to her. "I know, but that's what you look like today, a scrubbed child with her hair pulled back, fetchingly dressed in those pretty play clothes."

Was he being sarcastic? His smile belied that. It was pleasant, warm and appreciative. Apparently he was not going to bring up last night. Well, neither would she. He seemed so different from the dark and domineering man who had so ruthlessly exposed her own weakness to her. She was aware, though, that the other person was there beneath this amiable surface. He could be aroused again, she knew, and that thought was accompanied by a shiver of both fear and . . . anticipation.

"Thank you for the coffee. It was considerate of you to think of it when I missed breakfast."

"I thought you would need it as much as I did after a difficult night."

She panicked. So he *was* going to say something about last night. "I'll have to get moving if I'm going to meet Hercules for lunch," she said hurriedly, moving toward the door. "I don't want to miss another meal."

His face changed and his whole body stiffened. "No, you don't want to do that. Nor to miss any other pleasures your young officer may have in store for you, do you?" Without another word he walked back to his chair and picked up his book again. He didn't even say goodbye.

Well, that's O.K. with me, she thought as she turned and walked out. He hadn't mentioned his lecture, either. He probably didn't want her to come. Not that she cared. She'd go if she wanted to.

She strolled to the pool area, where she found Lisa stretched out on a deck chair talking to the two professors. Helen joined them.

"You three look lazy and quite content," she commented. "Aren't you going to dress for lunch?"

The men decided that that was a good idea and gathered up their belongings. "We've had enough sun," Lester Hayes said and cautioned Lisa about overdoing her sunbathing.

When they left Helen looked at her companion. "He's right, Lisa. There is a lot of you exposed," she said dryly.

It was true. Lisa was poured into a one-piece suit which barely covered the essentials.

"Too bad my efforts have been wasted." Lisa pouted.

Helen looked quizzical.

Lisa explained. "Here I donned my most revealing suit for the elusive Demetrios Criades and I haven't seen hide nor hair of him since breakfast."

Helen felt a sense of satisfaction. For some reason, which she didn't want to consider, she didn't tell Lisa that she knew where Demetrios was. "I'm meeting Hercules for lunch in a few minutes. Coming?" she asked instead.

"No," Lisa decided. "I've got other appetites on my mind right now." Helen didn't need to ask what they were. She quickly said goodbye and left.

Hercules was waiting for her in the dining room. Since the others hadn't yet arrived, they were alone. He greeted her with undisguised eagerness. "Last night I dreamed of the glamorous young woman I had been so fortunate as to meet. Today I am confronted with a ravishing young girl. Were it not that they are the same, I should be torn."

"Hercules, you're a terrible flatterer." Helen smiled. "But I love it." She did, in a way. Hercules didn't confuse her. He demanded only her acceptance of his attention and belief in his growing devotion.

He entertained her with funny stories about the curious events which occurred on cruise ships. He was reluctant to engage in more serious conversation, even when they were joined by the two professors and the older couple. Neither Demetrios nor Lisa appeared.

"Let's skip dessert so we can have our swim," Hercules suggested to Helen later, and they excused themselves.

"Perhaps we'll see you at Demetrios's lecture this afternoon," Lester, one of the professors, added as they were leaving.

"What lecture?" Hercules asked when they were outside.

"Oh, apparently Dr. Criades is delivering a talk on 'The Greek Temperament' today at four."

"Oh, good," Hercules said with relief. "I will be on duty." Then he laughed. "I am not very interested in dry, old lectures by dry, old professors."

"Demetrios is hardly old. He's not much older than you," she protested.

"That is true," Hercules admitted thoughtfully. "But he is certainly dry. This afternoon I want to get wet—with you—in the pool. You can go to the lecture later. It will keep you occupied when I am not with you."

When Helen went to her cabin to change she hesitated between the two bathing suits she had brought along. There was the daring and skimpy bikini she had bought in New York and her plain, pale blue tank suit. Remembering Lisa in her revealing suit, she almost reached for the bikini. But then she changed her mind.

She was not out to compete with Lisa in skin exposure or anything else, she thought as she donned the tank suit. She would make that apparent to Lisa and to anyone else who might . . . who just might . . . be with her.

Helen's righteousness was dampened when she arrived at poolside. No Lisa. No Demetrios. Just a broadly grinning Hercules, the subject of several admiring female glances as he sat by the edge of the pool waiting. She could understand their admiration. In a brief white suit, Hercules was all bronze, wide-shouldered muscularity.

"How pale I am next to you," she said as she took off her gauze cover-up.

"That will change quickly. As a matter of fact, we must be careful you do not burn. The sun is very strong." He seemed to be using the pronoun "we" more often.

"There's not much of me showing," Helen observed. "I feel positively prim."

"Prim . . . ?" When Helen explained, he commented, "I prefer modesty in a lady. The woman should reserve her charms for one man."

"Now you sound prim." She giggled. She wondered if he would have approved of her yellow bikini.

The sun was hot and the water was refreshing, even though it was heavily chlorinated and a little tepid for her taste. No matter. Soon she would be swimming in the Mediterranean and Aegean Sea.

They swam, enjoying the water, splashing, talking, teasing each other until she was tired. She left the water and Hercules soon followed. Helen felt his gaze grow more ardent as he watched her drying her hair with a towel. She realized that her tank suit, although it covered her slender curves quite adequately when dry, molded and outlined her body in a most revealing way when wet.

For some reason she suddenly looked up. There on the sun deck above them stood a dark figure inappropriately dressed in a white shirt, tie and brown suit. He was staring down at them, watching impassively as Hercules took the towel from her and started rubbing her tousled hair. Caught off balance, Helen almost fell over into the pool. Hercules caught her just in time. He continued to hold her, saying, "See, you need me to watch over you."

"It was you who made me lose my balance," Helen laughingly reminded him. Then, more loudly, she continued, "And I really don't need *anybody's* protection." Had Demetrios heard? She looked up. He was no longer standing there.

When she saw Demetrios again at four o'clock he looked different. He was wearing the same clothes, but his face wore a new look, animated, interested and friendly. She had walked into the small auditorium where his lecture was scheduled and found that a sizable audience had already gathered.

Demetrios was standing in front of the room, the center of an animated group which included the Graysons and the two professors. Helen hoped to slip unobtrusively into a back seat without being noticed when she heard Amelia Grayson calling her.

"Helen, there's an extra seat here. Join us."

Demetrios stepped up to the platform. The audience was getting into the seats. What could Helen do? She could not ignore the invitation, so she soon found herself seated in the front row almost directly in front of Demetrios. He seemed not to notice her presence as he began his address.

Helen had to admit that he was a dynamic speaker. She had expected him to be pedantic. He was not. His delivery was relaxed and confident. He was serious, yet he sometimes lightened the content with an amusing anecdote. The audience was totally absorbed.

Demetrios discussed the Greek temperament from a historical perspective. He described the demands history had made on the Greek people from ancient times to the present. There were three recurrent themes, Helen noted, pride, independence and love. She paid special attention to his conclusion.

"Thus we see that the Hellenic version of love, or *agape,* is all-encompassing. It includes family love, friendship for strangers, or *philoxenia,* personal friendship and romantic love, or *erota.* I hope all of you will have the opportunity to enjoy the Greek manifestation of *philoxenia.* Perhaps some of you may even find *erota.*" He looked directly at Helen, erasing her hope that he hadn't noticed her.

After some appreciative laughter and a great deal of applause he asked if there were any questions. A portly, elaborately dressed woman asked, "Dr. Criades, you describe the attribute of *philoxenia,* yet isn't it true that some tourists have encountered hostility?"

"I'm sure it is." He did not hedge or apologize. "It is true that there are rude people in Greece as there are everywhere. However, Greeks generally respond in kind. When they are treated with respect, they return it twofold. If they are patronized by a high-handed tourist, they withhold their friendship. And . . ." he continued ruefully, "some of us, especially the men, I must admit, may be a little hostile if we feel demeaned. We have a combination of patriotism and chauvinism we haven't completely controlled yet." His smile, so charming when he wanted it to be, thought Helen, took the edge off the words.

"Then you don't think we'll encounter any problems?" the woman persisted.

"I don't know," he replied a little impatiently. "There is a psychological basis to the idea that mental set can influence outcome. If you expect friendliness and warmth you're likely to find them. If you expect hostility you're likely to engender it. If you expect and desire quaint ethnic displays you will confine yourselves to guided tours and the main avenues of large cities. If you wish to feel comfortable you will seek Americanized Greek people who will remind you of home. However," and now Helen was certain he had a special message for her, "if you wish to have a true experience of the country, go to the side streets, to the markets, to the villages and the small islands. Take a bus instead of a limousine, a ferry boat instead of a cruise ship. Then you will discover something true about the people, and perhaps yourself."

In the usual way people gathered around the speaker afterward, asking questions and expressing appreciation. Amelia Grayson commented, "He really is a most interesting speaker, isn't he?"

Demetrios joined them a few minutes later, several members of the audience following in his wake.

"Congratulations, old man. Most enlightening," Mr. Grayson remarked in greeting.

"Especially your closing comment," someone else said, "about discovering something about yourself as well as about the new people one meets."

"I must give credit to another for that remark," Demetrios told them. "It was made recently by a young woman who planned to go to Greece to live and to work. However, I'm not sure she feels the same way anymore. She seems to have become more interested in American-style romance."

He was detestable! Tears of anger came to Helen's eyes and she darted out of the auditorium before they could fall. She, too, had been moved by his words and had felt herself responding to his message and, even more so, to him. Then, with words that had the force of a blow, he had managed to destroy that feeling.

Outside in the corridor she steadied herself against the wall. She refused to cry. She could not allow him to manipulate her emotions this way. Whenever she was ready to reach out to the sympathetic Demetrios, an antagonistic Demetrios took his place and slapped her down. He had said in his speech that hostility engenders hostility. That was the way she would play it, then.

Helen would not let him spoil her pleasure. Her remaining time on shipboard was full of activities. She and Hercules swam and sunned themselves, played deck games with other young people and danced every night. She developed a healthy tan, a new repertoire of dance steps and a basic Greek vocabulary, the latter a result of daily lessons given as part of the cultural offerings. Lisa joined in the festive parts of the schedule, sometimes cajoling a reluctant Demetrios to take part.

When he was with them Helen kept her equanimity. Indeed, she prided herself on being very polite, cool and detached to Demetrios. That this pride was often accompanied by an empty feeling was a price she was willing to pay. While she refused to give him much attention in person, she found that she could not keep him from intruding on her thoughts when she was alone.

Each day Helen found some time to be by herself, both through choice and because of Hercules's duty schedule. He would have monopolized her time completely if he could. She used some of the time profitably to study from the Greek workbook which was given in the course. Lisa teased her about doing "homework" when she could be vacationing.

"I wish I could be as disciplined as you." The other girl sighed. "Maybe if I appeared more serious Demetrios would take me more seriously."

"Do you want him to?" Helen asked.

"Unfortunately, yes. And obviously my charms alone aren't doing the trick. Perhaps I can convince him I'm on a self-improvement kick and he'll want to help."

During the remaining days of their trip Helen kept track of her roommate's progress. Demetrios still evaded Lisa's attempts to make them a twosome and didn't often join in their activities. Still, when he was present, he seemed quite attentive to Lisa, Helen thought.

With Helen, his attitude was one of sardonic amusement, as if he recognized her resolution to keep him at a distance. Perhaps he was amused by it.

Even when he wasn't with them, he seemed to hover on the periphery of her activities. She often found him nearby when she was at the pool, the lounge or the library. He was also constantly in her thoughts.

She became accustomed to taking a brisk walk after breakfast, then settling into a deck chair for an hour of study before her morning Greek lessons. Looking up from her book one morning, she was startled to see before her the face she had been trying to banish from her mind.

"You seem quite engrossed," Demetrios said as he sat, facing her, on the edge of the adjacent deck chair. "Love story?"

Was he being sarcastic? "No," she answered. "Unless you call my love for the Greek language a love story. I'm studying."

He raised his brows. "I'm impressed."

"I'm not trying to impress you."

"Someone else then?" The sarcastic note was back.

"No one," she snapped. "I'm doing this for myself. If I'm going to be living in Greece for two years I'd like to learn the language. This is a start, at least."

"I think there is much you need learn." His voice grew softer. "But you will not find it in a book."

"And where will I find it?"

She allowed herself to look directly at him and felt her anger softening. His gaze enveloped her, transmitting warmth and melting her coldness in spite of her resolve. Had she been misinterpreting his feelings?

"In people," he said simply. "Books are useful, but learning to read people is more important—and not only for the traveler."

"Well, I would expect you to feel that way. You're a psychologist. That's your profession, analyzing people." She gestured with her book and it slipped from her nervous hand.

They reached simultaneously to get it and Demetrios's hand covered hers. Their bent heads were close together, his eyes exerting an almost physical pressure, his mouth close to hers.

"I'm not speaking as a professional, Helen," he said, and his breath caressed her lips though he spoke so softly. "I'm not thinking as a professional. I'm not feeling as a professional."

She felt an inner trembling. She mustered her resolve, tore her eyes from his and sat up again. She tried to keep her voice from revealing her inner turmoil. She would not give in to her feelings. This man was so enigmatic; he confused her with his moods.

"Reading people, as you phrase it, isn't always easy." She was slightly breathless. "Some men— some people, that is—are too difficult to read. They change quickly and . . ." She stopped. His face had changed. He looked beyond her and his eyes narrowed as he watched someone approach.

"And other men offer less difficulty, is that it?" he asked as Hercules reached them. The blond officer knelt with a proprietary air beside Helen's deck chair as he smiled his greeting.

Demetrios rose without acknowledging the other man. His parting comment to Helen was, "Be careful. You might be misinterpreting messages which appear deceptively simple. You could get yourself in trouble." He turned and left.

"What was all that about?" Hercules inquired.

"Oh, nothing," Helen replied untruthfully.

"Strange man, that Dr. Criades," Hercules decided.

Helen agreed. He seemed able to elude everyone, including Lisa Rhodes. On their last night out, as they were packing in their stateroom, Lisa admitted that she had made no headway.

"Helen, that is one very difficult gentleman," she declared. "My only solace is that I really didn't have enough time to work on him."

A little harshly, Helen asked, "Did you expect the trip to end with a shipboard wedding?"

"Not a bad idea, but no." Lisa grinned. "I didn't really expect to get him to the altar. I couldn't even get him to my bed."

Helen was stunned by Lisa's frankness.

"Sorry, didn't mean to shock you. I keep forgetting what a sheltered life you've led, Helen. Yes, I sure did try. I've got to admit that my pride is a bit bruised."

"Just your pride?"

"For the moment. I wish I knew if his refusal was based on too much moral principle or too little desire."

Helen wondered, too.

Their arrival in Piraeus was accompanied by the same confusion, noise and crowds as their departure from New York had been, but this time the accents and commotion had a Greek flavor. Helen felt like a different woman this time. She could hardly believe that only nine days had elapsed. So much had happened during the brief voyage.

Had she handled herself appropriately? she wondered. She had encouraged the pleasant relationship with Hercules and, as much as possible, avoided further troubling encounters with Demetrios. There had been no repetition of that disturbing incident on deck the first night out. What else should she have done? It had, she insisted to herself, worked out as she had wanted.

On the pier, goodbyes were being said and addresses exchanged. "But where is Demetrios?" someone asked, voicing the question Helen herself had been thinking. "We have to say goodbye to Demetrios."

Could he have just gone off? It wouldn't be unlike him, Helen thought. She had difficulty maintaining her smile.

"Oh, there he is," Lisa announced, waving frantically.

He was walking toward them with two other people. Helen recognized the man as Jess Leigh; the woman must be his wife, Allison.

Jess greeted her warmly. "Helen, welcome! It's so nice to see you again. Demetrios tells me you had a great trip."

Helen darted a glance at Demetrios, but his face was expressionless.

Jess continued. "What a marvelous coincidence, both of you on the same ship. It gave you an opportunity to get better acquainted."

Helen smiled thinly.

"This is my wife, Allison," Jess introduced the smiling woman at his side. She was in her thirties, tall and rangy, with boyishly cut brown hair, freckles, and a wide grin. Helen liked her instantly.

Demetrios introduced Lisa and the others to the Leighs, who welcomed them all cordially.

"I know you'll enjoy your visit. Everyone does," Allison promised. "Although not everyone becomes as enamored as we have and just stays on and on."

She laughed, then turned to Helen. "You're staying with us tonight. Jess can help you find your own place tomorrow."

Helen tried to protest. She didn't want to be a bother, but Allison overrode her objections.

"Nonsense. It's settled. We have a spare room and it's all ready for you, and for your friend, if you like," Allison added, looking toward Lisa.

"Thanks, but I'm all set," Lisa announced. "I have an apartment off Syntagma Square, now minus one former husband. Like me, it will assume a new identity, bachelor digs for a bachelor girl. You all have the address, right?" She said "you all" but she looked only at Demetrios, Helen noted.

The goodbyes resumed again, with the usual hugging and kissing. Helen felt a strange tension; then a stab of excitement tore through her as she heard a voice at her side.

"So, here we are again with the farewell kisses." Demetrios's voice was low, so no one else could hear.

She stiffened with apprehension, then felt herself trembling with another emotion.

He moved to face her. "It has been a long time between kisses," he whispered.

Helen could not move away. She feared to look at him, both for what she might reveal and what she might see. Would he have that teasing, sardonic look, so intriguing but devoid of affection? He took her chin in his hand, as he had done twice before, and raised her head close to his. As she gazed into those commanding eyes, all her hard-won confidence and resolution drained away. She waited, unable to avert her eyes, oblivious to the others, feeling herself quiver inside.

Then, with a sudden motion, he dropped his hand. "But I forget myself." His voice was different, cool and public. "You have assured me you do not wish to invite such attention—not from me."

Helen felt as if she would fall over. She had been such a fool! Someone called him and Demetrios turned away.

Hercules came hurrying up to her. "Helen, I have to go back aboard now, but I shall call you tomorrow and we will . . ." His voice droned on and Helen nodded without hearing. Gently, but possessively, Hercules kissed her goodbye. She felt Demetrios watching and she was more upset than she cared to admit.

That feeling persisted as she rode with Allison and Jess to their home.

"I can't get over you two being on the same ship," Jess was saying. "I hope you had a chance to become well acquainted."

"We were all a pretty congenial group." Helen's reply was noncommittal.

"I got the impression that Lisa is quite anxious to improve on that acquaintance," Allison commented dryly.

"I didn't notice, but why not? He's an attractive guy. It's time he thought about getting married again," Jess added, then said to Helen, "I knew you'd change that first impression once you got to know him, Helen. He's quite a guy."

Helen was silent. She was grateful that she was sitting alone in the back seat, grateful that they could not see her face.

Innocently, Jess persisted, "Don't you think so, Helen?"

"Yes," she managed to choke out, "quite a guy."

Chapter Four

What fortunate people the Leighs were, Helen decided the next morning. Their house, although not large, was modern, comfortable and airy. Large windows and sliding glass doors opened onto the terrace from almost every room. They were kept shuttered during the heat of the day, then thrown open at dusk to catch the first light evening breezes. The use of marble, which she later grew accustomed to seeing in most Greek homes, lent coolness to the interior. But it was the outside which really delighted her.

The little garden surrounding the house was filled with fig, orange and lemon trees and many roses, now blooming profusely. The scent of the roses had filled her room when she first awakened and she had gone to the window to admire again the beauty of the garden she had been too preoccupied to enjoy fully the night before. The sight that greeted her was breathtaking. The Leighs' house had a commanding view of distant hills, almost mountains, dipping down to an azure sea now glittering with the rays of the morning sun.

How could anyone be troubled in such a world? she wondered. So what if Jess had shocked her deeply yesterday. He had used the word "again," said that it was time Demetrios thought of marrying "again." After all, Demetrios's past history should not be her concern. He had made it obvious that he thought very little of her.

Of course, an unhappy former marriage might explain his attitude toward women. He might have been hurt in the past. Helen couldn't help wondering about the woman who might have caused his bitterness. How long ago had he been married? Had Jess and Allison known her? What had happened? Helen had all she could do to keep from raising the topic at breakfast.

As a special treat, Allison prepared a typical American breakfast, orange juice, scrambled eggs and bacon, toast and coffee. "The only item easy to come by was the eggs," she said, proud of her feat. "I had to really scrounge for the sliced bread and the bacon. And the prices! It's lucky that Jess and I have gotten used to Greek foods."

"You shouldn't have gone to so much trouble for me," Helen protested.

"Nonsense. I enjoyed it. Besides, we don't want you to go through too much culture shock your first day. You need time to get used to new foods and new customs."

"What is a typical Greek breakfast?" Helen asked.

"Hard-crusted, but delicious, bread, with cheese or honey and hot milk. Sometimes a soft boiled egg," Jess replied. "It's really fine, except for the hot milk. That's one habit I haven't adopted."

"One of the few," his wife fondly commented. "Sometimes I think Jess has become more Greek than American. He even picked up the *'thsuh!'*" Allison clicked her tongue on the upper ridge behind her teeth and threw her head back.

"What is that?" Helen laughed.

"That, my dear Helen, is something you'd better get used to. To a Greek, it means 'no,' an emphatic 'no,'" Jess said. "What looks like a nod, when accompanied by that sound, is a negative; a slight shaking of the head to one side is 'yes.' A young, unmarried woman had better make sure she knows which is which. Otherwise, she could get into a lot of trouble, especially romantic trouble."

"Not much chance of that," Helen assured them. "I'll have too much to do learning the language, seeing the country and getting ready for school in September."

"There's *always* time for romance," Allison insisted.

"Quite right!" agreed Jess. "And from what Demetrios told me, you already got a head start on board ship with that young officer."

So they had discussed her! When? Their only opportunity had been before they had joined the others on the pier. Demetrios had apparently wasted no time before criticizing her behavior to the Leighs.

"Dr. Criades should mind his own business. My friendship with Hercules Phyllos is none of his affair," she said sharply. "What did he have to report?"

"Helen, don't take it that way." Jess tried to

mollify her. "He certainly wasn't 'reporting.' He's just concerned that you may be getting yourself too involved too quickly without really knowing this man."

"I am *not* involved."

"That's the problem," Allison pointed out gently. "You may not think so, but Hercules may have different ideas. Helen, young people here have different . . . what shall I say? Mating habits. Men divide women into two categories, those they go to bed with and those they marry. They avoid the latter like the plague until the time is right for them to marry."

"And what constitutes the right time?" Helen asked.

"Career security for one, and such old-fashioned traditions as having married off all your sisters and finding a bride with sufficient dowry." Jess smiled at Helen's surprise. "Yes, I said dowry. Greece is quite modern, especially in the cities, but some old customs still persist."

"Well, don't worry. Hercules hasn't asked me about my bank account yet," Helen said flippantly.

"There are the two categories, Helen, and Demetrios wasn't sure which one Hercules had placed you in. He was afraid you didn't know what you were getting into."

Helen became angry. "I know what I'm getting into. And it's none of his business."

"I'm sorry you feel that way," Jess said. "I had hoped you would have changed your first impression of Demetrios. If anything, being together on the Olympia seems to have complicated the matter."

He was right, Helen admitted to herself. The

more she saw of Demetrios, the more complicated her feelings became.

"Don't let it trouble you," she said. "My attitude toward Dr. Criades won't interfere with any professional relationship we might have. And I'll certainly be careful if we should meet socially." Helen tried to laugh lightly. "If we see each other here, I don't want you to think you'll have to act as referee. I know Demetrios is your friend."

"I don't think we'll see much of him for a while. I expect he'll be going to the village." Jess turned to his wife. "Did he say, Al?"

"No, but I expect he'll be gone for part of the summer, anyway. We'll probably find out this afternoon." Allison noticed Helen's sudden alertness. "He's going to come by after *siesta.*"

Helen's head buzzed with questions. Why does he go to what village? Exactly what time would he arrive? The one she asked, however, was the safest and the least important to her. *"Siesta?* Do you have *siestas* in Greece?"

"Absolutely," Allison affirmed as she started to clear the dishes. "It's a civilized and intelligent custom."

Jess suddenly became efficient. "Come on, Helen; let's get started before Allison puts us to work. We'll check out some of the apartments on a list of vacancies I have. Then we'll stop by the school. I have to pick up some papers and you can look over the campus."

"Leave time for a swim, either before or after *siesta,*" Allison interrupted. "I'm sure Helen will welcome one after dragging around with you all day."

"Hey, dragging around with me is a privilege, not an ordeal, lady." Jess gave his wife an affectionate hug. "Hasn't done you any harm and you've been dragging around with me for years."

Helen went to get her bag. How nice it was, she thought, to see two people tease each other in such a good-natured, loving way. The words didn't matter, she knew. It was how they were meant.

She heard the ring of the telephone. "Helen," Allison called a minute later, "it's for you. Hercules."

Hercules practically shouted his news. After a few more days of duty he would be free for a while and could devote the majority of his time to Helen. He was on his way to meet the ship in Piraeus, but wanted to stop by to see her for a few minutes first. He was disappointed when she said she was on her way out and even more displeased when he heard of her mission.

"An apartment? But you are not to live alone! I thought you would be staying with Mr. and Mrs. Leigh."

"That's just temporary. I want my own place."

"But it is unseemly, Helen. You will come to us." He paused for a second, then, pleased with his suggestion, continued, "My mother and sister will love to have you. They are already eager to meet you and planning a dinner party of welcome. A young lady alone . . . no, it is not right. You must stay at our home."

He meant well, of course, but Helen found herself resenting his attitude. Why did everyone try to tell her what to do?

"That's out of the question. I lived alone back

home and, unseemly or not, I intend to have my own place here, too. I really must run now. Talk to you later." She ignored the disappointment in his voice as he rang off, promising to call that evening.

Jess was efficient and cheerful as they drove around town following up various apartment leads. Helen realized what a difficult time she would have had without him. She'd have to learn the bus system and maybe even pick up a car after she got settled. In the meantime, Jess was a godsend. He knew the streets and neighborhoods and spoke the language. He translated for her, haggled with the renters, and usually managed to get the quoted annual rent reduced by twenty-five percent before he was through.

"Bargaining is traditional," he explained. "It's part of the fun. There's no such thing as a firm price except in the large stores. If we actually took the first price quoted, the landlord wouldn't know what to do. I'm sure he'd feel guilty."

All the apartments they looked at were in the suburb of Psyhiko. "So you'll be near the school, near us, and out of the heat and bustle of downtown," Jess explained. Helen was grateful for his advice, but still unsure what to do when they finally stopped for a cool drink at a small sidewalk cafe. The apartments were nice, spacious—and empty. The idea of signing a two-year lease on an unfurnished apartment, which she would then have to furnish, overwhelmed her. It seemed too much of a commitment too soon.

"What do you think?" asked Jess. "Did any of them please you?"

She explained her reservations. "I just don't think

I'm ready for this yet. I hoped for a small, furnished place. I know you said that's hard to come by, especially in the summer, with all the tourists here."

"They're also pretty seedy. If you're concerned about the expense, Al and I are pretty good bargain hunters."

"It's not just the expense. There's also the time and effort involved. I just feel 'not yet.' Everything is still too new, and I have so much on my mind."

Jess became sympathetic. "Of course. You've hardly had a chance to catch your breath and I'm showing you real estate. Why don't you just relax and use our place as a base for the summer? I know I speak for Allison, too, when I say we'd love to have you."

"I couldn't think of it. I'm sure I can find a hotel room, pension, or something for the time being."

Jess thought for a moment. "Wait," he exclaimed. "I have the perfect solution. Mrs. Caratides!"

"Mrs. Caratides?"

"She's a widow. Lives in a nice, large, older house not two blocks from here. Right outside the school campus, as a matter of fact."

"Does she rent rooms?"

"Not usually, but Anastasia, that's her daughter, just graduated from our school. I helped her get into college back in the States and she's going to spend the summer with my folks in Vermont. She left last week. You can take her room."

"Just like that." Helen smiled at his assurance. "How do you know that Mrs. Ca—"

"Caratides," he furnished.

"—Caratides even wants a boarder?"

"Because she said just last week that she was

68

lonely and Anastasia had only been gone for two days." He stood up and beckoned the waiter. "Come on. Let's go see her. It's a perfect solution. Perfect!"

When Helen met Bertha Caratides she was inclined to agree. Mrs. Caratides was a robust woman with dark hair and shrewd eyes. She was obviously very fond of Jess, but looked Helen over somewhat suspiciously when Jess explained his perfect idea. Without committing herself, she took them up to see the large, airy, second floor bedroom, coolly shuttered against the midday heat.

Helen admired the polished wood floors, the old-fashioned, marble-topped dresser, the sturdy bed with its brightly patterned coverlet.

"Oraia," Helen exclaimed. *"Poli oraia."* She was trying to say "Very lovely" and hoped she had it right.

Bertha Caratides was won over. Her eyes lost their coldness and a wide smile graced her olive-skinned face as she repeated, *"Oraia?* Pretty? You like. *Kala!* Good!"

Later Jess congratulated Helen on her diplomacy. "That was the perfect thing to do. Speaking the language, even only a few words at first, shows you're really trying to understand the people. They're really turned off by high-handed tourists."

"I wasn't trying to be diplomatic. Not consciously. I really did like the place—and the woman."

"I hope you have as good a first impression of our school."

Jess needn't have worried. Helen was delighted when she saw the campus with its low, white, limestone buildings and spacious grounds. She was surprised, however, by the absence of grass. Then she realized that she had seem almost no lawns in the residential sections, either.

"It's too dry," Jess explained. "It almost never rains in the summer and Greeks consider it wasteful to squander water on lawns. Precious water is reserved for trees and flowers and fruit. I must confess that, after years in America worrying about fertilizer, crab grass and lawn mowers, I don't mind one bit. Of course, you're going to get a little dusty as you walk around."

He was right. She left Jess in his office while she took a quick tour. As she walked, her shoes raised low clouds of dust on the unpaved paths. In front of the Administration Building she knelt to brush the dust from her shoes. Suddenly she noticed a shadow, the long shadow of a man, approach. She didn't look up, but she knew it wasn't Jess. Then the voice confirmed the identification her racing blood had made.

"At work so soon. Jess must be a hard taskmaster."

She raised her head reluctantly, hoping that Demetrios—for that was who it was—wouldn't notice her loss of composure.

"Why, hello." She hoped she sounded casual as she stood up, smoothing the skirt of her light summer dress. "No work today, just a quick tour of the campus. What are you doing here? Were you looking for Jess?"

"No, I just stopped by to see a friend." He turned. "Here's Jess now."

"Demetrios," Jess greeted his friend. "I didn't expect to see you until this afternoon. What's up?"

"I just stopped by to see Alexandra. Maybe take her to lunch."

"Alix is working in the library this week," Jess informed him. "It's about time for her to be quitting now."

Who was Alexandra? Helen couldn't help wondering. Then she heard Demetrios ask, "How was your morning? Did you succeed in your search for an apartment?" He obviously knew more about her activities than she did about his.

"Sort of. There was a change of plans," Jess answered. "Helen didn't feel ready to sign a two-year lease right away."

"And why not?" Demetrios directed his question to her. "Isn't your contract for two years?"

"Yes, it is. But it seemed like such a big step. Signing a lease, buying furniture . . ."

"Making a commitment?" Demetrios offered with a rising inflection.

"Making a commitment," she repeated without thinking, then checked herself. "No, I don't mean that. I have a two year commitment to my job. But the apartment was just too much, too fast." Again he had succeeded in making her sound defensive.

Jess cut in. "Helen, I think you're quite right. After all, Demetrios, she just got here. And we've found the perfect solution. You remember Anastasia Caratides? Well, she'll be in college in the States and Helen will rent her room here. That's our own personal exchange program. Don't you think that sounds good?"

"Yes, if one wishes to postpone commitment and be able to pick up and leave at one's whim." His voice was cool, his eyes critical as he looked at her.

"Whim! That's hardly an appropriate term. You make me sound like some kind of irresponsible dilettante."

She reddened when he didn't refute her.

"Cut it out, you two," said Jess with his usual good nature. "Helen, you said I wouldn't have to referee, remember?" Demetrios looked uncomprehending as Helen nodded with some embarrassment. "And here's Alix," Jess said as he waved to someone, "so if you insist on arguing, you'll have to finish this afternoon."

Helen turned quickly to get a look at the woman who was able to command Demetrios's attention as soon as he arrived in Athens.

But it wasn't a woman at all! Amazed, Helen looked at the young girl who had just come out of the library and was running toward them. She was about twelve, thin, almost fragile, with delicate, classic features, gray eyes and silky, straight, light brown hair.

"Demetrios, you're back!" the girl exclaimed joyfully, practically flinging herself into his arms.

Demetrios hugged her, then swung her off her feet as she giggled with delight. Then he held her away from him and took a long, penetrating look. Helen had never seen such an expression on his face before; it reflected joy and humor and love. It transformed him.

"Of course I'm back. And how is my girl?" He smiled at her, still holding both her hands. "You look thin. Have you been eating properly? Your grandmother will scold you."

"I eat and eat, but I just get taller instead of fatter. Soon I shall be as tall as you," Alix quipped, taking in his six-foot figure.

"You've still got a way to go," Jess said. "Alix, this is Miss Stathos. She'll be teaching English here in September."

Alexandra flashed a wide smile. "How lovely! Can I be in your class? Are you married? Do you live near here?"

Helen was amused at her eager rush of questions. "I'm very pleased to meet you, and I certainly hope you'll be in my class. I'm not married and I'll be living right by the campus, at least for a while." She shot a glance at Demetrios.

"Then I shall come to visit you," Alix declared. "I have Demetrios, but it will be so nice to have a lady friend, also."

Helen was captivated by the girl, so eager one moment and so wistful the next. Who was she to have been so befriended by Demetrios?

"I would enjoy that very much," Helen told her.

Jess mopped his brow. "It's getting too hot standing around here. Allison's waiting lunch for us. You two want to come?"

"Thank you, no. Alexandra and I have a private date. We have much to talk about since I have not seen her for several weeks. Tell Allison I'll be over about five."

"She's expecting you. Bring a suit. We'll go to Vouliagmeni for a swim before dinner."

"Very well. Let's go, little one. *Adio.*" Demetrios strode off with Alexandra skipping along beside him, clinging to his hand.

"What a lovely little girl!" Helen remarked, hoping Jess would pick up the cue and tell her about Alexandra's relationship with Demetrios.

"Yes," he agreed, "she's a nice youngster."

She tried again when they were in the car. "How

come Alexandra is on campus during the summer when the other students are gone? Is that usual?"

"No. Alix's grandmother had business to attend to in Switzerland, so she asked us to keep Alix on at the school for a while. She'll be back in a couple of weeks and then she'll probably take her on a vacation trip, as she usually does."

"It must be terrible being in the dorm alone."

"She's not living in the dorm. She's in that cottage, next to Dr. Brady's, with Jessica Mills, the librarian."

"She must be lonely, though."

"I guess she is sometimes. Jessica is a very nice lady, but she must be fifty-five or sixty. It just happened that she was spending an extra month on campus to reorganize the library so she asked Alix to stay with her. She and Alix are really fond of each other. Alix even helps out in the library. I guess there's not too much else for her to do. Jessica is hardly an exciting companion for a twelve-year-old."

He said no more and Helen didn't want to question him further lest he wonder at the extent of her interest. She didn't feel the same reluctance with Allison, however.

After a leisurely meal, Jess retired to rest while the two women cleaned up.

"Alexandra said she's going to visit me," Helen mentioned.

"Oh, I'm glad. I know she's lonely at times."

"Well, now that Demetrios is back, perhaps she won't be," Helen ventured.

"That's true," Allison agreed. "But she needs feminine companionship as well."

"They seem awfully close," Helen probed. "Isn't that an unusual relationship?"

74

"Yes and no." Allison's reply was enigmatic. "Didn't Jess tell you about her background?"

"No, and I didn't want to pry," Helen lied.

"Well, you'll hear sooner or later. It's common gossip. But there's still a lot of mystery surrounding Alexandra. Her mother died ten years ago. She was raised by her grandparents, who lived in Switzerland. Then, last year, her grandfather, Nikolas Likakes, died. Her grandmother brought Alix to Greece and enrolled her in our school."

"Nikolas Likakes? Wasn't he a famous ship owner? Fabulously wealthy, too, I think I read."

"That's the one," Allison confirmed. "Alix is the only heir. Someday she'll be a wealthy woman."

"But what about her father? Isn't he involved in her care, or did he die, too?"

Allison gave her a peculiar look. "Nobody knows."

Helen had a strange feeling, almost fearful. What was Allison omitting from the narrative? "What's the mystery?" she asked.

"I may as well tell you. You'll hear the gossip soon enough. The rumor is that Alix's mother, Chrysanthe Likakes, had been married briefly to a Greek student. Her father had disapproved. She was underage; the boy was penniless. Her father took her away."

"But what happened to him, then? Who . . . ?" Helen stopped, stunned by her sudden realization. "You mean Demetrios . . . ?"

Allison nodded. "At least that's the rumor, and there's enough evidence for me to believe it." Demetrios never brings up the subject, and no one has the guts to ask him point blank."

"But doesn't Alix . . . ?"

"No." Allison had anticipated the question. "She believes her parents are both dead. Demetrios is simply her beloved friend whom she met at the school and just idolizes."

So that's it, Helen thought. No wonder Demetrios had treated Alexandra with such love. She was his daughter!

Retiring to her room for the afternoon *siesta*, Helen tried to sort out her turbulent thoughts. She needed to make plans. She wanted to move her things to Bertha Caratides's home tonight, or tomorrow at the latest. Then she wanted to make summer travel plans, and she had to check into the books and resources available at the school and sort out the materials and unit plans she had brought from home. And then there was Hercules. He had said something about a dinner party his family had planned. But her mind rebelliously refused to deal with these questions.

Instead, she kept seeing Demetrios as he had appeared that afternoon with Alexandra Likakes. The hardness of his face had melted as he spoke with the girl. Could he ever look at her like that . . . ? She couldn't dismiss the disquieting idea which made her breasts heave under her filmy nightgown. Did the child remind him of the mother? Did his love for the girl substitute for his love for the woman he could not forget? Finally, in the coolness of the shuttered room, she dropped off to sleep.

An hour and a half later Allison thumped on the door. "Come on, get out of bed and get your bathing suit; Demetrios is here."

Helen got up quickly. She couldn't believe it was almost five o'clock. Where was her bathing suit? She rummaged through her suitcase. There was the yellow one, the scandalously brief suit she had bought on impulse. Where was her tank suit? She rummaged through again. With exasperation, she noticed the mess she had made, all the piled clothing.

Oh, what's the difference, she decided. I'll wear the yellow. After all, I did buy it for Greece.

She put it on and surveyed herself in the mirror above the bureau. Even standing on her toes she could see only part of her body, but it wasn't her legs she was worried about. Had she added weight on the cruise? The bathing suit didn't look or feel tight, but it revealed a lushness she hadn't remembered. She slipped on a sundress over the suit, grabbed her bag and a towel, and went out before she lost her nerve.

The others were waiting on the terrace. Demetrios had not changed from his suit, but he had removed his jacket and tie.

"You look like you're going to a business meeting instead of the beach," Helen remarked. "Aren't you going for a swim?"

He showed her the rolled towel he held. "This is all I need. A towel and my suit. I'm sorry I don't please you."

Helen was determined not to argue. "But you do," she said, and then blushed. "I mean, it doesn't matter what you wear. I mean . . . oh, let's go to the beach." She ended up laughing at her own embarrassment.

They went to Vouliagmeni, a public beach about twenty minutes north of the city. "It's more of a drive, but less crowded than Astir Beach," Jess explained as he turned the car into the parking area. "The water's cleaner, too. Much better for swimming!"

When Helen saw the locker arrangements, she realized why the others had carried their suits. For a nominal fee you were given a locker and could change, leave clothes and valuables, then shower and change to street clothes later.

When she took off her dress she felt self-conscious and timidly threw her towel over her shoulders when they emerged to join the men. She spotted Jess and Demetrios walking over from the men's area. It was the first time she had seen Demetrios informally attired. She tried not to stare as she took in his bronze, sinewy body and brief blue trunks. Where, she wondered, had he acquired such a deep tan? His stomach was flat, his chest strongly carved and dusted with curly brown hair. When he looked at her, she averted her glance as if caught in a gesture of intimacy.

Jess, stocky and solid in brightly printed trunks, spread the blanket and immediately headed for the water. Allison, whose white, two-piece suit enhanced her rangy, athletic form, sprinted after him.

"Come on, you two," Jess called from the water's edge. "This is what we came for."

"Coming," Helen called. Self-consciously, she dropped her towel. She felt Demetrios's eyes explore her body, his gaze as palpable as a touch. She walked toward the water, trying to ignore the eyes which followed her. Then he was there beside her, unexpectedly taking her hand and urging, "Come on."

"No," she hung back, "not so fast. I can't just race in."

"This is not like the cold North American waters," Demetrios said, pulling her slightly. "Here there is no shock. The waters are warm; they caress your body, as, indeed, it deserves."

Helen felt herself grow hot. She pulled away, running to the water lest he see in her body the response she could not control. She took a shallow dive, rose, and started swimming out to Allison and Jess.

"Hey, slow down," Jess advised. "We swim in a leisurely fashion here. You act as if you were pursued by the devil."

Perhaps she was, Helen thought as Demetrios caught up, swimming effortlessly. Still, she could not help but enjoy the water. The four of them swam quite a distance, talking very little, just relaxing in the pleasure they felt.

When they returned to the beach Helen dried her face, rubbed her hair briefly, then enveloped herself in her large beach towel before she sat.

"Helen, you'll suffocate. It's so warm," Allison cautioned.

"I'm all right. I'll just dry myself this way," Helen said. She saw a slight smile tugging at the corners of Demetrios's mouth.

"We won't be here long enough to get completely dry. But we'll change out of our wet suits before we go to dinner," Jess commented.

"Change? But I didn't bring anything." Helen was dismayed. "I thought we'd get dry just sitting on the beach."

Demetrios's smile widened. "Then you had better take that towel away and let the sun dry your suit. It shouldn't take long considering how little fabric there is."

"Demetrios, don't tease," Allison scolded. "You're embarrassing the girl."

Stonily, Helen sat, refusing to remove the towel. Later, in the locker room, she was sorry. Her bathing suit still felt clammy.

"It's still damp," she said to Allison. "Me and my modesty!"

"Take it off," her friend advised. "Your dress is a cotton print and quite opaque. Nothing will show."

"Oh, I couldn't!"

Allison shook her head, then suggested, "Compromise. At least take the top off. You'll be much more comfortable."

Helen hesitated, then gave in. Allison was right. She felt better getting out of the wet bra and hoped the rest of the suit would dry quickly.

When she and Allison joined the men waiting for them by the car Helen felt Demetrios's eyes on her. He seemed to be examining her closely.

"Do I look all right?" she asked Allison in a whisper.

"Perfect. No problem."

"Then why do I feel half-naked when he looks at me?"

"Who, Jess? I'll kill the cad!" Allison pretended alarm. Then, seeing Helen's consternation, she relented and advised, "Stop worrying. He's looking at you in an admiring way. How *you* feel is something else again."

Over dinner, Helen gradually lost some of her self-consciousness. They drove along the shore to a restaurant in Phaleron where the tables were set at the water's edge. Demetrios had taken charge, she noticed, choosing their table and conversing animatedly in Greek with the waiter. She was surprised when Jess and Demetrios stood.

"Come on. Let's choose our supper," Jess said as he and Demetrios started walking back to the kitchen.

Allison explained as they followed the men. "It's the custom her. You can go into the kitchen and look into the pots and see what looks good to you."

"How unusual," Helen noted. "Imagine asking to go into the kitchen of a restaurant back home. You'd probably be thrown out."

"I know, but here it's expected. This place has great fish. That's probably what I'll have."

Since Helen loved fresh seafood she was happy to take Allison's recommendation, especially when she saw how the fish was ordered. Freshly caught fish were laid out on a bed of ice. You pointed out the one you wanted. The cook weighed it and told you how much it would cost. He asked if you wanted it pan fried or grilled and then proceeded to cook it for you. They each chose a fish and Demetrios took care of the rest of the order. While Demetrios was doing this Helen wandered about the kitchen, taking delight in the delicious aromas coming from the large pots on the burners. A short, heavy woman with a wide smile obliged by lifting the lids and allowing Helen to peek at the simmering contents. She named each one for Helen: *giuvetsi, dolmades, bamies, moussaka.* The names were as exotic as the aromas. "You want?" she would ask each time, and never seemed offended when Helen said no.

Helen was so engrossed that she had forgotten about the others until she noticed that Demetrios, having finished ordering, was looking at her with an indulgent smile. "Do you wish to try some other dish?" he asked.

"If I were to sample everything that looks inviting, I'd burst," Helen answered. "I just enjoy looking."

"So do I," he said, looking at her.

"Obviously," Allison told him wryly, "but save some of your appetite for dinner."

Helen thoroughly enjoyed the dinner. While they waited for their fish to be grilled, they relaxed with a bottle of retsina, a distinctive Greek wine. Helen's first sip made her frown at the strange taste. The others laughed.

"That's the usual first reaction," Jess assured her. "The resinated flavor is new to the American palate, but you'll probably find you develop a taste for it."

Helen wasn't so sure. She was glad the Greek cheese and bread adulterated the taste at first. However, as they talked, she found herself sipping the wine and beginning to relish its dry, unusual flavor. Soon her glass was empty.

"See, I told you," Jess laughed, filling it again.

"But you should also continue to eat with the wine," Demetrios advised. "With wine and ouzo, one should always have something to eat."

Helen noticed that the waiters always brought a dish of feta cheese, bread and olives whenever they brought drinks to a table.

"That's why you seldom see many drunken people here," Allison claimed. "They never drink without eating. And, speaking of eating, here comes our main course."

The fish, simply grilled with oil and butter, was the best Helen had ever tasted. It was served whole. Demetrios deftly showed her how to cut around the head, split the fish in half and cleanly remove the center bone. He nodded approval as she, somewhat more clumsily, prepared her fish.

"A very good first attempt, especially after only one demonstration. I see you learn quickly."

"Only with a good teacher," Helen said.

Jess raised his hands in pretended amazement. "I can't believe you two are actually complimenting each other." He raised his wine glass. "Well, here's to friendly relations."

The others joined the toast. "I certainly approve of close relations," Demetrios added, capturing Helen's eyes with his own.

Helen had never seen him so relaxed nor felt more relaxed in his presence. The haunting questions she had harbored earlier were forgotten—for now.

Chapter Five

It had been such a pleasant dinner. Helen was sorry when Jess, looking at his watch, declared, "We'll have to get going. It's late and Mrs. Caratides is expecting Helen tonight."

On the way home she and Demetrios sat in the cramped back seat. The windows were open to let in the cool evening breeze. Helen leaned back, closing her eyes. She felt a slight, but pleasant, giddiness which she attributed to the retsina. Fortunately, Demetrios did not feel the need to talk. Talking might spoil the unusual harmony they had enjoyed this evening. She was dimly aware of Jess and Allison whispering very quietly in the front seat.

When they arrived at the house Allison turned to Demetrios with a request, "Jess is feeling a little tired, so would you mind taking Helen over to Mrs. Caratides's? Keep the car to drive home and drop it off tomorrow."

So that's what they had been hatching! Helen started to protest that she could move the following day, but Demetrios cut her short. "Of course you'll go tonight; the lady is expecting you. I don't mind at all." He said he would take her over that night with some of the luggage, and then Jess would take care of the rest the following day.

Helen put what she would need immediately into one suitcase and they left. It was a short drive, and she was almost sorry when he stopped in front of the Caratides's house. Demetrios took her bag out of the car while she reached into the back seat for the beach towel she had left there. When she pulled it out it unrolled and the top of her bathing suit fell to the ground. Demetrios reached to retrieve it. He dangled the bit of cloth from his finger, an amused look on his face.

Helen was unreasonably flustered. "I forgot I had it rolled up in the towel."

"Such a little thing is easy to forget," he drawled, handing it to her. "I'm sure you were more comfortable not wearing it."

She became unbearably conscious of how little she was wearing under her sundress. When she heard Mrs. Caratides's voice coming from the porch, it was a welcome distraction.

"Miss Stathos?" the older woman called. "Come, come, I wait."

Bertha Caratides greeted Demetrios by name and with a great deal of respect, as well as pleasure. Apparently they had met before. The two of them carried on a lively conversation in Greek as they entered the house and climbed the stairs to Helen's room.

Mrs. Caratides opened the door, proudly announcing, "Is ready. I fix for you today."

Helen walked in and smiled her approval at how nice the room looked. Demetrios followed with her bag. "Thank you so much," she said gratefully as Bertha Caratides beamed. The landlady then bid them good night and departed, closing the door softly behind her.

The way the door had been closed imparted an intimacy to their being together. Helen was afraid to meet his eyes. When he spoke, his voice was low. It, too, suggested intimacy.

"I think Mrs. Caratides was trying to be discreet, leaving us alone in your bedroom this way."

Trying to appear cool, she lifted the suitcase, intending to put it on the bed. "How foolish," she said in what she hoped was a light and steady voice." Does she think that we . . ." Caught off balance by the weight of the valise, she dropped it on the bed as she tripped sideways. Demetrios reached and caught her arms, steadying her. Then his hands moved around to her back, their warmth penetrating through the fabric of her dress.

"Not so foolish, I think." His voice was soft and slow as he pulled her against his body. "She may have read our desire better than we." His head came down and he kissed her bare shoulder, then her neck, then, lingeringly, the soft valley between her breasts. His hands caressed her back, which was bare above the low-cut back of the dress.

His mouth was fiery, enflaming every spot it touched. She had no time to think, no time for resistance. When his mouth covered hers all thoughts of resistance evaporated in the heat which enveloped her.

Her arms were on his shoulders, then about his neck, then pressing his head closer. He explored her face with his lips, caressing her eyes, her brow, her ear, her upper lip, then, with intensified passion, her mouth again. An answering passion surged through her. When she felt him slowly pulling down the zipper of her dress, then touch the small of her back before dipping below to the rise of her hips, she could offer no resistance.

She knew she should. One careless touch, and the dress would drop, leaving her almost naked in his arms. With an effort, she pulled her head back, trying to speak, her mouth moving against his. Interpreting her movement as passion, Demetrios bent her back more fiercely as he renewed his embrace.

"Miss Stathos! Helen!" The voice jarred them. Demetrios raised his head but still held her.

"Miss Stathos, *telefono*. A call for you." Coming from the first floor, Bertha Caratides's voice finally penetrated Helen's consciousness.

"Hercules Phyllos, he says."

Helen pulled away from Demetrios's grasp. "I'm coming," she called. The sound of her voice was strange to her, hoarse and choked.

Demetrios stepped back, his face suddenly masked with the impassive coldness it often wore. "Of course," he said sarcastically. "You would not want to miss such an important call."

"Is there any reason why I shouldn't take the call?"

"If you see no reason . . ." He shrugged; then he surveyed her coldly. "But I suggest you . . . uh . . . adjust your clothing first."

Helen became instantly aware of her still trembling body, her unzipped dress, the straps loosened and falling down her shoulders, the top of her dress lowered and barely covering her breasts. One moment longer . . . If Mrs. Caratides had not called . . . Was Demetrios thinking the same thing? She redid her zipper and adjusted her dress.

"I . . ." she began, "I don't want you to think . . ."

"What?" His voice was like a shot. "What don't you want me to think? That you were ready to give yourself? That you wanted me to take advantage of you?" He made the last four words heavy with sarcasm. "That you don't have as much control over situations and over yourself as you claim?"

"You mean . . ." she sputtered in outraged disbelief, "you mean that you deliberately set out to prove that I could be . . . taken advantage of?"

He did not answer.

Her voice became firmer as she grew angrier. "You are the most arrogant, egotistical and . . . cruel man I have ever met."

"Not like the wonderful Mr. Phyllos?"

"Not at all like him! How ironic that you should be warning me about him. He would never attempt . . ." She couldn't finish.

"Of course, he would. He's a man, is he not? And you're a little fool." With that Demetrios turned on his heel, left the room, went down the stairs and out of the house.

Helen followed in a daze. Hercules was still on the line. He talked on and on, telling her that Jess had passed on her new number. His words hardly registered with her. His mother had invited her for dinner on Wednesday, he said. He assumed that was all right. He would pick her up at seven; Mrs. Caratides had given him the address. He was glad she would be living in someone's home. He missed her. How did she feel?

Apparently Helen gave the proper, if short, responses, because Hercules seemed quite satisfied when he said good night.

As Helen hung up Bertha Caratides eyed her sympathetically. She had apparently sized up the situation and reached her own conclusions. "Two is too much," she told Helen with a wise shake of her head. "One is best. You take one man only. Dr. Criades, he need you."

Helen fought back her tears. "Dr. Criades doesn't appear to need anything or anyone. And I don't need him." She ran up the stairs and closed herself in her room.

That night she relived the episode over and over again in an agony of anger and self-disgust, anger at Demetrios and disgust at the memory of her own desire.

He had been playing with her, demonstrating his control. What would have happened if Bertha hadn't interrupted? She shivered.

Hercules was so different. He was uncomplicated; he didn't twist her thoughts or upset her tranquility. She tried to concentrate on him, on the prospect of a pleasant evening with his family, her first visit with a Greek family. But the lines of his face blurred into the image of a dark and brooding portrait.

"Don't know what was wrong with Demetrios," Jess commented the next day when he brought over all her luggage. "He brought the car back early and took off. He wouldn't even stay for coffee." He looked at her curiously, but she didn't react at all and he left her to her unpacking.

She was grateful for the activity and tried not to think of anything but what she was doing. When the last bag was unpacked, the last book put away, and her papers sorted, she sat on her bed. What could she do now? Jess and Allison would be coming to dinner; Bertha had invited them and he had said he never turned down the invitation from her landlady, who he called the best cook in Athens.

Well, Helen decided, she certainly wasn't going to sit in her bedroom all day and brood. It was only eleven-thirty. There was a lot to see and do in Athens, so she might as well start. Armed with a map of the city she went downstairs to ask Bertha about buses.

She found Mrs. Caratides at the front door talking to someone who had apparently just arrived. Helen's pulse quickened, but, no, it was not Demetrios. It was, however, someone close to him. Alexandra Likakes greeted her merrily.

"Miss Stathos, I have come to visit, as I said. Oh, you are going somewhere." Her disappointment showed.

"I was on my way out," Helen admitted. "I was going to take the bus into town and explore Athens on my own for the first time. But that can wait."

"No, no. I shall go with you. I do not have to go back to the library this afternoon. I shall be your guide—that is, if it is all right?" Again she displayed that charming combination of eagerness and wistfulness. Helen couldn't resist.

"I would consider myself fortunate," she informed the delighted girl. Mrs. Caratides offered to call the librarian so Miss Mills would not worry about Alix and off the two went.

Alix, Helen realized, was a most adept guide. She had apparently spent a lot of time on her own, though she was still young. She knew all the bus routes and, when they walked in the city, all the streets and public buildings. Taking great pride in her role as a teacher, she pointed them out to Helen.

As they rounded a corner, Helen saw the Acropolis in the distance. It was more awesome than she remembered. She stopped short, causing Alix to look at her quizzically.

"I first saw that sight many years ago with my father," she explained. "I was just about your age. I've never forgotten how beautiful it is!"

"I know," Alix agreed. "I have come on school trips, but it's best when I come with Demetrios. He knows all the stories and he loves to go there. Do you want to go now?"

"No," Helen decided. "It's afternoon and very hot. That visit deserves more time, starting early in the morning. Today I'm just going to let you guide me around Athens. We'll just walk. O.K.?"

And walk they did, with Alix chattering every inch of the way, from the sophisticated cafés and hotels of Syntagma Square to the bustling business area of Omonia. Alix pointed out the bus terminals; they looked at public buildings; they ventured in and out of shops. Crowds thronged the streets. "It is the resting time," Alix explained, reminding Helen that here, as in other Mediterranean countries in the summer, everything closed down at 2:00 P.M. and reopened at four or five. Despite the government's attempts to change it, the Greeks stubbornly clung to that tradition.

Helen was beginning to appreciate why this was so. The afternoon heat was so excessive that, after walking for two hours, she was ready to drop. Alix responded with enthusiasm when she suggested that they stop for something to eat before going back to their suburb of Psyhiko.

"Oh, yes, we'll go to Vasili's, where Demetrios takes me; it's very near. And we shall have *dolmades*. Won't Vasili be surprised when he sees me two days in a row?"

Vasili, the owner of the little open-air restaurant, was indeed surprised and happy to see Alix again. He smiled indulgently as she introduced Helen. "Vasili, this is Helen, Miss Stathos. She is Demetrios's friend, and now she is my friend, too."

"Then she is a friend to Vasili as well," the man replied with a smile. The meal he served them lived up to Alix's praise. The *dolmades*, savory meat and rice rolled up in tender grape leaves, were topped with a tangy lemon sauce. Demetrios's name came up several times in the course of their conversation, but Helen resisted the temptation to ask Alix questions about him. She wondered, though, if she would ever be able to escape him, at least while she was in Greece.

Later, at Mrs. Caratides's house, Alix was invited to stay and have dinner with them. She and Helen helped Bertha Caratides in the kitchen. Bertha, as she asked Helen to call her, obviously enjoyed the company. She said that she missed her daughter Anastasia and it was nice to have someone to talk to. Helen found that, with Bertha's broken English and her own newly learned Greek expressions, they communicated very well. Where there was a difficulty, Alix delightedly translated.

"You see how good I am as an interpreter. But soon Helen will not need one. She learns very fast."

Alix complimented her pupil, and they both laughed at the reversal of their roles.

"I'm learning from both of you," Helen said. She was busily crumbling some white feta cheese into the salad. "If I watch you, Bertha, I will learn how to prepare all sorts of Greek dishes. This is a very elaborate dinner."

This was too much for Bertha, so Alix translated. The woman beamed. "Too bad Dr. Criades not come," she said. "He go to village."

Helen stiffened.

"He'll be gone only a few days," Alix offered. He goes back and forth all summer, to see his mother and to pick up some of his things. He says funny things sometimes, Helen."

"Oh?"

"He says the visits to the Acropolis revive his spirit and the visits to the village refresh his body. I'm not sure what he means. I like them both when Demetrios takes me. Are you sorry he's not coming to dinner tonight?"

"Uh . . . yes, I guess so," was Helen's faltering reply. She ignored Bertha's knowing smile. So Demetrios had been asked to dinner! Was her landlady trying to play Cupid? Apparently it was going to be hard to avoid him in Athens, but she intended to do her best. Whenever they had been alone together he had made a fool of her. She would not give him the opportunity to do so again.

She spent the next day at the school with Jess, where he went over her program and described her assigned classes.

"I don't understand why you want to do this now," he commented. "There's plenty of time in

September before school starts. You should be relaxing."

"But I like doing this," she insisted. "And, naturally, I'm curious about what's in store for me. I want to make sure I'm prepared for my assignments."

"Oh, I have no doubts about your preparedness for your *work*." He placed his emphasis on the last word.

She acknowledged the implication. "But you're not sure about my preparedness in other areas? Is that it? I see Demetrios has influenced your judgment of me."

"Not at all. But I must admit, I'm not sure you realize what you're getting into. I don't presume to give you advice, but . . ."

"But . . . ?"

"It's just that accepting a dinner invitation to the Phylloses' may be rushing things."

"A simple dinner?" Helen was unconvinced.

"That's the point, Helen. It may not be a simple dinner. I don't know these people but, in Greece, when a young man's mother formally invites a young woman to dinner it's a serious business. He's probably announced his intentions to them, so they're going to look you over. If they approve, it's considered an established fact."

"What's considered an established fact?"

"The betrothal," Jess declared with mock pomposity. Then he became serious again. "Look, Helen, a casual visit would be different, but this sounds like a very formal occasion."

"But that's ridiculous." Helen dismissed the notion. "I've only known Hercules for about two weeks. I know he likes me, and I think he's very nice, but that's all, at least for the present. Tonight is just going to be an evening in a Greek home with a Greek family. That's what I'm looking forward to, not a betrothal."

"That's what you think," Jess retorted.

The events of the evening proved that Jess was right. It was obvious that the whole family had been summoned. Hercules proudly introduced her to the assorted relatives. Dismayed, she realized that she was indeed being assessed as a potential addition to the family. It became an ordeal for her to answer all the prying questions.

I wonder if they'll inquire about my bank account, she speculated, then scolded herself for her ungraciousness. After all, they were following their own customs and trying to be hospitable.

But the whole evening was a disappointment. Instead of an evening in a typical Greek home she found herself the guest of honor at a South Elmsford type dinner party, even to the pre-dinner cocktails and roast beef. The visit dragged. Pleading a headache, she asked Hercules to take her home early.

On the way home, Hercules was solicitous. She didn't feel like talking, so she just let him go on; he told her about the various people she had met, people whose names she could no longer remember. When they reached the Caratides house she said tiredly, "I hope I didn't appear rude."

"Of course not," he assured her. "I understand. Meeting my whole family at once . . . it was not easy." He smiled indulgently. "But, since this is serious, Mother thought it wise."

"That's just it, Hercules. I'm afraid they, and you,

have the wrong impression." Then, very gently, she proceeded to set him right. She was sorry, but he had misunderstood. His expectations, and now his family's, were premature. He looked crushed.

"It's just too soon," she said with frustration. "Everyone expects me to accept commitments too soon. I couldn't even bring myself to sign a two-year lease the other day. How can I make a lifetime commitment so quickly?"

Hercules was contrite. He hadn't meant to rush her or to presume too much. They would get to know each other better, although he could not imagine changing his mind. Even his mother had agreed that Helen would make a most suitable wife for him.

She cringed at the word "suitable," but he didn't notice and continued. Although they had known each other but a short time, he said, he could see that they were well-matched.

"You are sweet and lovely, a lady. I shall take much pleasure in spending time with you to convince you to spend your future life with me. You will see how suited we are. You will not be sorry."

Were they suited? Would he think so if he had uncovered that passionate streak in her which seemed to surface at Demetrios's bidding? Was she foolish to want more from marriage than comfort and suitability?

For the next ten days she tried to put Demetrios out of her mind. It should have been easy, since he was not around, but it wasn't. Through Alix and Allison she was aware of his comings and goings. He had gone to the village. He had picked up his car and returned to his Athens apartment. He had resumed his practice and hospital work. He had gone to Salonica for a two-day Psychological Association conference. He was back.

When he was in town he saw Alix often and visited the Leighs occasionally, but Helen always seemed to just miss him. It couldn't have worked out better if she had planned it, she told herself. In fact, it was almost as if it were planned. Perhaps he was as determined to avoid her as she him. Inexplicably, the thought annoyed her.

Her days were spent pleasantly enough. Hercules was in constant attendance, although she refused to let him dominate her time. He kept transmitting invitations from his mother, but Helen avoided a repeat visit. She made time for studying her Greek, which she practiced on Bertha, who was delighted with her progress. She had dinner with the Graysons and met Lisa one day for lunch. Alix was a frequent visitor. Helen often included the girl in her outings, to Hercules's chagrin. And she saw the Leighs frequently, since she and Allison had become good friends.

Jess urged Helen to make some travel plans. The tourist season was at its height and reservations were becoming difficult to arrange. For some reason, she was reluctant. This pleased Hercules, who interpreted it as a desire to be with him while he was in port.

One day Allison asked, "Is Hercules the reason you're putting off traveling?"

"Of course not." The immediacy of her response had the ring of truth.

"Is there another reason? Someone else you don't want to leave?" Allison was gentle, but not very subtle.

Helen didn't answer at once. "Who else could there be?" she finally asked.

"Answering a question with a question is just a stall," Allison admonished.

"Then, yes, there is. I don't want to leave you and Jess; so there." Helen tried to turn it into a joke, but Allison would not be put off.

"Look, I know something happened between you and Demetrios the night he took you home."

Helen felt the blood rush to her face.

"Whatever it was, he looked stone-faced when he came back with the car. He absolutely refused to stay over when I suggested that he help Jess deliver the rest of your things after breakfast. 'She won't want to see me.' That's all he said and then he stalked out." She paused, but Helen did not react in any way.

"I thought I was doing the two of you a favor, giving you the chance to be alone. But I guess I blew it. . . . Or he did. . . . Or maybe you did!" Helen still said nothing.

Allison threw up her hands. "I don't know what's with you two. There's something between you, but you're succeeding admirably in avoiding each other, and Jess absolutely forbade me to interfere."

"There's nothing between us," Helen finally said. "He obviously has no more interest in seeing me than I have in seeing him." Her words had more conviction than she felt.

She didn't resent Allison's interest. She valued her friendship, and Jess's, as well. But they were wrong about Demetrios.

The American School was sponsoring a weekend bus excursion to the ancient theatre at Epidaurus. Jess thought it would be a good opportunity for her to meet some of the other faculty members in an informal way. Helen thought it would be a good opportunity to get away from Hercules, whose constant presence was becoming trying, so she accepted gratefully. Allison seemed especially delighted, more than the occasion warranted, Helen thought, then decided she was becoming too suspicious. It would be nice to get away.

Chapter Six

Helen had assumed that Jess and Allison would be on the excursion to Epidaurus, so she was surprised when Allison claimed a prior commitment.

"But don't worry. You won't be lonely," Allison predicted.

That was a funny thing to say, Helen thought. Of course she wouldn't be lonely. There were over a dozen teachers signed up for the trip.

The bus was to leave Friday evening for the trip to Nauplion, the seaside town where they would be staying. On Saturday they would proceed to Epidaurus, where they would attend an evening performance of an ancient drama. Sunday morning they would be free to let them enjoy the sights or the beach at Nauplion. Then, that afternoon, back to Athens.

The group met at the school parking lot where they were to board the bus. The other teachers, a few of whom Helen had already met, represented an assortment of types from various parts of the States. They were mostly young, exuberant and single.

She enjoyed the bus trip, which took them past Corinth and Tiryns, where they stopped for a fast visit. It was hot and dusty, although very interesting. Helen looked forward to relaxing after dinner and turning in early, and turned down the others' invitation to check out the local nightlife.

The next morning dawned with almost unreal beauty. Helen was awakened early by the sounds of the fishermen getting ready to go out for the day. Some of the others had complained that the little hotel in Nauplion was situated right on the wharf, but Helen was delighted with the setting. The sea reflected shades of azure and gold, and the sky was a deeper blue, and totally cloudless. By mid-afternoon, Helen knew, a heat haze would blur the sharpness, but right now the picture was perfect.

She leaned far out of her bedroom window, her eyes devouring the beauty of the morning. A young fisherman, his attention caught by the movement, looked up at the pretty young woman in the flimsy nightdress leaning over the window sill. He grinned appreciatively.

"Kalimera, koukla," he called insolently. She couldn't help but smile at the words which, she knew, meant "Good morning, pretty one." He was tanned and muscular, with dark, curly hair and a healthy, bristling moustache, perfectly cast in the role of a Greek island fisherman.

Her smile obviously encouraged him, for he came closer and called, *"Ela kato, koukla. Pame volta me to kaigue mou."* She knew enough Greek to recognize the invitation. "Come down. We'll take a ride in my little boat." Almost tempted, she laughed down at him before caution prevailed. The invitation, she knew, included more than a boat ride.

Helen moved away from the window, hearing first his disappointed cries of *"Koukla . . . koukla . . ."* then, scornfully resigned, *"Eh, na tourista."* What can you expect from a tourist?

Helen had to laugh to herself as she quickly dressed. If only she could react as simply as the fisherman. When something attracted him and seemed available, he admired and went after it. When the goal moved out of reach, he dismissed it. She envied him. But enough of that. Today was a carefree day. Why spoil it by philosophizing?

The group breakfasted at the hotel, sitting on a sunny patio overlooking the water. They gorged themselves on Greek bread, butter, honey, cheese and coffee.

"This honey is truly the nectar of the gods," sighed one young man as he contentedly licked a sticky finger.

"Well, they're wasting it on a peasant like you," countered his girl friend. "You've got it all over you. Wipe your mouth," she ordered, laughing.

"And deprive you of the opportunity to kiss my sweet lips?"

She threw a roll at him and the others laughed. In this lighthearted mood, the group boarded the bus for the day's outing.

The morning passed quickly and Helen marveled at the beauty of the mountains surrounding them and the villages in the Argive Plain.

They stopped frequently at places of interest, an archeological site, an old Byzantine church with ancient and beautiful icons, the remains of a classical temple with but a few standing pillars to indicate its ancient grandeur.

The young teachers listened with interest, often with awe, as Kyrios Constantinos explained the historical significance and pointed out the rare beauty at each stop. Kyrios Constantinos was also a teacher at the school, one of the few native Greeks on the faculty. Helen admired the elderly man; he seemed to know everything there was to know about Greek history and tradition. He taught world history but the history of his native land was his greatest passion.

After a plentiful midday meal of fresh grilled fish, a salad of tomatoes, cucumbers and feta cheese, and the sweetest watermelon she had ever tasted Helen found herself back on the bus, unable to keep her eyes open. The Greek tempo of life, with its afternoon *siesta*, was getting to her and she closed her eyes with a feeling of contentment.

It seemed as if only a moment had passed, although it had really been over an hour, when she was jarred awake as the bus rolled into a rocky, unpaved parking area.

"We're here," someone called and Helen smiled to see the many sleepy eyes, yawns and stretches as the group roused itself.

Although it was late afternoon the sun still blazed brightly, but it hung low on the horizon. The midday haze was gone; the sky was still cloudless and the mountains starkly beautiful. What a dramatic setting! No closed-in theatre could match it, no architectural embellishments could compare. The amphitheatre was only about one-third filled and Helen was glad. She wanted time to look around, to absorb the atmosphere of this ancient and sacred site.

Kyrios Constantinos led their group down to the orchestra, a perfect circle where the chorus would be situated, with the raised wooden stage behind. He explained the ancient theatrical traditions which Helen remembered from her own study of classical theatre. Then he asked them to climb to the highest row in the theatre to experience the remarkable natural acoustics. He remained below and, amazingly, they could hear every word he said quite easily.

The theatre was quickly filling up. During the fourth century, fourteen thousand spectators had filled these stands to witness the Greek dramas, religious rites sacred to Dionysus. The theatre could hold that same number today and Helen marveled at the crowds that were still attracted to ancient drama. Tonight the play was to be *Medea,* hardly light summer entertainment. Yet it looked as if all the places would soon be taken as the sun dropped lower still.

"So many tourists," Helen remarked to Kyrios Constantinos.

"Look again, Miss Stathos," he said. "At least half this audience is Greek. Some of the men have come straight from the vineyards. See the children? A number of them are barefoot."

He was right. On the stone tier below them a large family was filing through. It looked as if three generations were represented. A little girl of about nine, holding an old man by the hand, led the way.

"Come, Grandpa, here we are," the girl urged. Then there was the grandmother, with her black shawl covering her head, three other children, a swarthy, powerful man, who indeed looked as if he had been working in the fields that day, and his wife, a beautiful woman whose black hair was drawn back and knotted, exposing classic features.

"She's beautiful enough to be down there on stage, playing Medea," Helen whispered.

"You forget," corrected Mr. Constantinos, "the women's roles are always taken by men, just as in ancient times." He seemed about to go on, but then his attention was diverted. "Ah, here you are, Dimitri; I was afraid you would not find us."

Helen followed his gaze and was startled to find herself staring at Demetrios. She almost failed to recognize him. How different he looked! His face was more deeply bronzed and his hair was sun-streaked as well, giving him a tawny look. His whole appearance was vibrant with color and energy. When he saw them he broke into a wide smile and, with an easy grace Helen did not remember, moved to join them.

"But why?" he asked the older man. "This is where we agreed to meet."

So this wasn't a coincidence. Helen suddenly remembered Allison's remark. "Don't worry. You won't be lonely." Now she realized what Allison had meant.

Noticing her surprise, Demetrios asked, "Didn't Jess and Allison tell you I was coming up?" He looked at her and found his answer. "I guess not. I had an important conference this morning, so I took the public bus up after lunch."

"Demetrios has done this before and we have never failed to find each other," Kyrios Constantinos told her.

"I'm adept at such things," Demetrios said lightly, "especially when I'm so drawn by the attraction."

Demetrios looked closely at Helen. "I hope my unexpected appearance hasn't upset you."

"Upset . . . ? Of course not. Why should I be upset?" But she knew she sounded awkward, and she certainly felt strange. This new Demetrios was disturbing, and more attractive than ever. He wore a blue sport shirt, open at the neck, white denim slacks and leather sandals. The casual attire suited the rugged aspect he had acquired, just as his somber clothes had set off the sarcastic look he had worn with them. "I just didn't know that this kind of performance was of interest to you," she finished awkwardly.

"Did you think Epidaurus was only for tourists, Helen? We Greeks enjoy our ancient drama."

She flushed. She had sounded patronizing and he had put her in her place.

Demetrios sat down between her and Kyrios Constantinos. His thigh brushed her own and his proximity reminded her of the last time she had been close to him, in her room. Was he remembering that scene, too? She didn't think so. He seemed so cool and relaxed, while she felt hot, disheveled and confused.

At first she was grateful when he turned to speak to Kyrios Constantinos; it gave her a chance to compose herself. She deliberately forced herself to breathe slowly, regularly, so she wouldn't sound so nervous when she spoke again. After a few minutes, however, she felt neglected. Then she became impatient. When would he look around again?

"What time does the play start?" She realized her question sounded curt. Still, it served its purpose; Demetrios turned back to her.

"Whenever the sun goes down, which should be very soon," he answered. "It is, you know, in Greek, but I don't think you'll have difficulty in following it. It's *Medea.*"

"I know. I've read the play."

"I believe that this drama is as well known in America as in Greece. It appears that the anger of a woman scorned is universally understood."

"Do you think these people in the audience really know the plot?" Helen sounded skeptical.

"I presume you're not referring to the tourists," he said. She had, apparently, done it again. He was amused, but some of his former sarcasm had returned, as well.

"Helen, 'these people,' as you call them, grew up with the ancient tragedies. They may not have studied them in the classroom, although I'm sure some did, but they know them as part of their heritage. They understand them with their blood and their hearts."

Ashamed, Helen started to explain that she hadn't meant to sound so patronizing when she became aware of a hush in the crowd. The sun had gone down beyond the mountains, leaving a russet glow to outline the stark peaks. As if at a signal, the people quieted, settling into their hard, stone seats. She, too, allowed the hush and the deepening darkness to envelop her. She, too, drew her breath sharply when the first figures appeared. She gave herself up to the drama unfolding below, feeling the moaning of the chorus, the tragic anguish and hatred of Medea, and the pride of Jason. Now she knew what Demetrios had tried to convey. She couldn't understand the ancient Greek dialogue, but she understood the feelings, as he had said, with her heart and her blood.

At the point when Medea, unseen, killed her children, the horror of the event caused Helen to reach over to Demetrios without thinking. He clasped her hand and she left it in his, hardly aware that they were joined in a shared emotion. The drama continued to its inevitable tragic conclusion.

At the finale, there was no immediate applause. Collectively, the audience allowed itself a silent sigh, a drawing back from the intensity of what they had experienced. Then the applause started, spreading to a crescendo. It finally subsided and the audience, brought back to the reality of the present, started to stir.

Two voices penetrated into Helen's consciousness as she heard Demetrios and Kyrios Constantinos expressing their admiration of the performance. She turned to join their conversation, to voice her own pleasure at the experience. Only then did she become aware that her hand was still firmly clasped.

"We'd better be going," she said, withdrawing her hand and covering her confusion with practicality.

She started down the stone steps and was quickly surrounded by the hordes of people all trying to leave the large amphitheatre.

She didn't look back to see if the others were following close behind her. She simply followed the crowd, let herself be drawn by it out to the parking area. There she stopped, bewildered. There were so many buses. Which was theirs? Where was their group? And where was Demetrios? Suddenly she saw him emerging from the crowd and let her breath out with relief.

Demetrios pushed his way to her and took her by the arm. "You shouldn't have run off like that," he told her sternly. "We lost sight of you for a moment." Had he been anxious?

If he had been anxious, that anxiety had faded quickly, Helen decided. He didn't even sit close to her on the bus ride back to Nauplion. Would he also choose to avoid her at the supper which awaited them back at the hotel?

When the bus stopped in front of the hotel Helen delayed getting up until Demetrios reached her seat. Then she stood and stepped in front of him.

When they got off the bus it seemed perfectly natural for them to walk together to the dining terrace. Helen didn't think of her action as deliberate; it had just happened, she told herself. If she had intended to be alone with Demetrios she wouldn't have asked Kyrios Constantinos to join them at their table, would she?

Conversation was sporadic as they finished their supper of cheese, olives, salad and *moussaka*. The eggplant and meat dish, held together with a rich bechamel sauce, had become one of Helen's favorites. Demetrios smiled as he watched her wash it down with a glass of retsina.

"So you have learned to appreciate our local wine. I remember how you reacted that first night in Piraeus."

Helen laughed as she recalled her initial distaste. "I know," she said. "It's an acquired taste, I guess, as are many Greek dishes."

"Food only?" Demetrios inquired. "Or does that extend to . . . other things?"

Kyrios Constantinos looked from one to the other

with amused puzzlement, then folded his napkin and stood. "I think it's time for me to go to bed; you two can stroll on the *paraleia* and continue to confuse each other." His smile was indulgent. *"Kali nikta,* good night, my friends."

"Well," Demetrios said after the older man left, "we shouldn't disappoint him. By all means let us stroll on the *pareleia* and confuse each other."

"And what is this *pareleia?"* Helen asked as she allowed herself to be led out.

"Every town has one; it's the place where one walks in the evening. The old people sit and watch the young amble by. It may be around the town square, or its main street, or, as here in Nauplion, along the shore, which is the best."

He grabbed her hand to pull her out of the way of a child on a tricycle, and continued to hold onto it as they walked silently. There was a pier, with benches, extending into the bay, and Demetrios led her along it. They sat next to a couple who had left room on the other half of their bench, but they were soon left alone as the young lovers disappeared into the night.

Demetrios laughed, his breath stroking Helen's cheek. "I'm afraid we've disturbed them," he said and squeezed her hand. Instinctively, she answered the pressure. His face came closer.

"You give your hand so nicely, Eleni."

She started to withdraw it and he protested. "No, I didn't mean to embarrass you, Eleni. It was a true compliment."

"You call me Eleni."

"That is your name in Greek, Eleni. It's softer, is it not? Somehow it seems appropriate tonight. Don't you like it?"

She raised her face to his and found his eyes inches from hers, his mouth a whisper away.

"Yes," she murmured just as his lips closed on hers. His mouth was gentle and remained so as his lips tenderly traced her own. He released her hand and drew her closely to him.

Helen found her lips responding, moving sensuously to explore the outlines of his mouth, parting at the probing of his tongue. Her hands were pressed to his chest, warm and pulsating beneath the cotton shirt.

His lips moved to kiss her eyelids, her temple, her ear into which he whispered, "Yes, so soft, and so sweet, so very sweet, Eleni," sending shivers she knew he could sense deep within her.

"Kita! Kita tous Amerikani," came a derisive voice. Two young men were walking by.

Demetrios drew away. The mood was broken.

"What did he say?" Helen asked.

Demetrios looked at her wryly. "He said, 'Look at the Americans making love.'"

She laughed nervously. "Well, they were wrong, weren't they . . . because you're not American, are you?"

"Nooo," he drawled slowly. His voice was gentle as he added, "I think we had better go back."

She knew he was right, but she also knew she didn't really want to go.

Helen didn't sleep easily that night. She lay on her bed, remembering the warmth of his body, the searching pressure of his lips. Desperately, she turned, burrowing her body into the soft mattress and her head into her pillow. Finally she slept.

When she went down to breakfast most of the

others had already dispersed to swim or fish or beachcomb. Demetrios sat at a table with Kyrios Constantinos. They both waved and beckoned when they saw her emerge from the hotel. So, too, did the young fisherman standing nearby on the pier. It was the young man from the previous morning, gazing at her with the same insolence.

"Eh, koukla, kalimera. Good morning," he called and repeated his previous morning's invitation to take a ride in his caïque. Helen ignored him and walked to the table. She smiled to herself as she felt his gaze follow her. She couldn't be angry and didn't even resent the teasing which greeted her.

"Our young native men have good taste, Helen," Kyrios Constantinos gallantly observed.

"I may have to fight him for your company," Demetrios quipped.

As it turned out, Demetrios found what he said was the perfect compromise. He hired the fisherman and his little boat to take them to a more secluded beach farther up the coast.

"That way we can share you," he said, then abruptly changed his mind. "No, I don't think I should like that. But at least he can look."

And look was all he did. The young fisherman resigned himself easily enough with the same kind of acceptance she had noticed the day before. He brought them to a beautiful little cove, deposited them on the beach, and promptly found a shady spot to fall asleep.

No longer inhibited about her brief swim suit, Helen allowed herself to relax completely. She and Demetrios lay on the sand, walked the beach and swam in the clear water.

"I thought the water at Vouliagmeni was lovely, but this is absolutely like crystal," she marveled as she swam easily with slow, almost languid strokes.

At her side, Demetrios commented, "Do you remember how Jess teased you about swimming as if you were being pursued by a devil?"

"Yes."

"You don't feel that way anymore . . . ?" It was half statement, half question.

Helen's answer was evasive.

"No, I guess I've adjusted to Greek time. I don't rush so much; I've learned to relax."

Yes, she thought, today the devil was absent. She floated languidly on her back, propelling herself by kicking slowly. Demetrios lazily circled her and she was conscious of his eyes on her. The water, eddying about and drifting over her, blurred the outlines of her body and made her movements seem more sensuous. She felt that way as well, conscious of the water drifting over her fingers and legs, the warmth of the sun on her face and midriff, her hair fanning out on the surface of the water, and the almost palpable touch of Demetrios's gaze.

Suddenly she felt a sharp pain in her left foot and cried out. "I think something bit me," she gasped, taking in a mouthful of briny water. "My foot . . ."

Demetrios grabbed her, supporting her with one arm about her waist while he raised her foot with his other hand.

"Stop flailing around," he ordered. "It was probably only a crab." He seemed to be laughing.

"What do you mean *only* a crab? A crab can take your toe off." She had expected a little sympathy.

"Not our little crabs," he insisted, now smiling

openly. "And your toe is not off. See?" He held her foot above the surface of the water. "All five—and quite intact."

Helen became very conscious of his hold on her. Where his skin touched hers she felt a searing heat, despite the coolness of the water.

He dropped her foot and circled her waist with his other hand, bringing her body even closer to his as they tread water. Startled by his sudden movement, she reached for his shoulders and his arms tightened around her.

"Is it the custom in America, as it is here, to kiss a hurt to make it better?" he asked softly against her ear. Then he kissed her ear, running his tongue across it lightly, inciting tremors deep inside her.

"Yes," she answered, struggling to keep her voice even, adding lightly, "but it's not my ear which is hurt."

"True," he breathed, "but I thought I would work my way down, a very delightful journey."

Helen forced herself to break away from him. "I think I'm all right now. I can make it to shore." She swam away quickly with purposeful strokes. Demetrios took off after her.

"I see the devil has apparently returned," he said sharply as they reached shallow water.

"I don't know what you mean," she replied, out of breath from her effort. She winced as she stood up and then cried out as she stepped onto the hard-packed sand with her injured foot.

Before she could protest Demetrios swept her up in his arms and carried her to the spread out beach towel where they had left their things. He stood there for a moment holding her, peering down at her, but she would not meet his look. Then he set her down so abruptly that she fell backward on the towel. Demetrios leaned over her. His face came closer, blotting out the sun behind him. His mouth touched her throat and moved caressingly, lingering at the hollow.

She shivered. "What . . . what are you doing?" she asked.

He raised his head a little so that his eyes were directly above hers. "Working my way down, as I said," he replied.

"Oh . . . please . . ."

"Please what? Tell me what you want." His voice was husky and impatient, and its harshness startled her.

What *did* she want? Her body, she knew, had its own answer, a trembling but insistent call for his closeness. She could not allow that.

"Come, you two!" They had forgotten about the boatman until his raucous voice startled them. From the shade of the tree where he had been reclining, he had been watching them with a combination of interest, envy and amusement.

"Let's go! *Pame!*" he called. "It is getting late."

Demetrios hovered over Helen a few seconds longer, his eyes hard. "Some day, Helen, you will have to answer that question," he said evenly, his voice normal again. "For now, our boatman has given you a reprieve." He stood and started to gather up their things.

Resentfully, Helen noted that he had been able to rein in his emotions very quickly. The teasing, warm sensuality had been replaced by a cool and subdued practical tone. Which did she really prefer? The first both thrilled and frightened her; the second left her feeling chilled and unsatisfied.

Still, she tried to quell her disappointment and even to emulate his mood of detached friendliness later on at dinner and on the ride back to Athens. If he could summon and subdue his emotions at will then she, too, could learn.

On the trip back, Demetrios persuaded the driver to make a side trip to Mycenae, mainly for Helen's benefit.

"You have read of the horrors which befell those of the House of Atreus. It will be interesting for you to see where it all took place."

The narrow road leading to the ruins was lined with eucalyptus trees and oleander. The austere, gray ruins themselves were an appropriate setting, she thought, for the tragic events in the lives of Agamemnon, Clytemnestra and their children. Kyrios Constantinos led them through the famous and imposing Lion Gate to the Acropolis of Mycenae. Later Demetrios guided a small group of stalwarts through the dark beehive tombs outside the reconstructed walls, holding Helen by one hand and a lantern in the other. His commentary was thorough, including both history and legend.

Back on the bus, Helen complimented him. "If you ever decide to give up your practice I'm sure you could earn a living as a tour guide."

"Thank you, though I meant to show off my country rather than my own erudition. Perhaps today I was doing both to impress you." His smile of self-deprecation was charming. "I promise to be more modest when we go to the Acropolis this week."

He noticed Helen's surprise.

"Allison didn't tell you? Apparently not, just as

she neglected to tell you I was coming on this weekend trip. Very forgetful of her, considering she made a special point of asking me to go along with you."

"Allison has a conveniently unreliable memory."

"I hope you don't mind." He looked at her closely.

"Oh, no," she said with complete truth.

"I hope young Lt. Phyllos doesn't object. He is to accompany you, too, no doubt." His voice was now somewhat cool.

"Yes . . . he is. . . . I'm sure he doesn't care; it's just a sightseeing trip." But Helen really wasn't so sure. She didn't want to think about Hercules now, though, and she didn't want Demetrios to think about him. She was glad when he dropped the subject.

When night fell the bus quieted and when Demetrios moved away to speak to the driver about dropping him off near his home, Helen closed her eyes drowsily.

"Helen, Eleni . . . Elenaki . . ." It was Demetrios, sitting next to her again, whispering her name in English, then in Greek, then in the diminutive, an endearment. She felt her heart pounding, her senses becoming instantly alert, but she forced herself to open her eyes sleepily. Demetrios put his arm around her, gently easing her head onto his shoulder.

"There," he whispered, his voice deep and soothing, "now you will be more comfortable."

She allowed herself to relax against him as his cheek dropped to touch her hair. Did he believe she was asleep? She felt hypocritical, faking sleep to be close to him this way, as if she knew the gentleness couldn't last. All too soon, the bus slowed and Demetrios gently disentangled himself.

He said softly, "The driver is letting me off here, near to where I live." She opened her eyes. His face was very close and she held her breath as he bent closer still. His lips just brushed hers, tenderly, undemanding.

The bus creaked to a stop. Hurriedly, he said, "I must get off." Then, quickly, he was gone. As the bus started to move she peered out the window at the dark silhouette walking away. Her eyes were wide open, straining. Did he turn and wave? It was too dark to be sure.

Chapter Seven

When Lisa called her the next day Helen was glad of her invitation to visit. Lisa's apartment suited its occupant—strikingly modern and colorful. The two girls sat on the terrace overlooking Syntagma Square and sipped iced tea.

"I don't know." The blond girl pouted. "I came here to sell the apartment and wind up my affairs, but I can't seem to get to it."

"Have you been that busy?"

"I wish I had been. I've called the elusive Demetrios a dozen times but I've only managed to see him twice. And then only briefly and publicly, for a drink."

"Oh." Helen tried to show only mild interest.

"I think he's afraid to come up here. He doesn't seem to believe my 'help me to reform' routine. Maybe I've come on too strong. He's probably afraid I'll compromise him. And he's right; I'd sure try," Lisa admitted.

"I don't think Dr. Criades is afraid of anything—

least of all any woman," Helen said, secretly pleased by Lisa's lack of success.

"Maybe you're right. He may just be too busy. I'm getting sick of being alone, though."

"What about your friends?"

"They were *our* friends, mine and Jeff's," Lisa explained. "Married couples, mostly foreign service people. Now I'm out of place, at least as far as the wives are concerned."

Helen could understand the reluctance to welcome back the now liberated and footloose Lisa.

"Maybe you *should* sell this place. Get rid of old memories and start fresh—back home." Helen denied to herself that she had any selfish reason for making this suggestion. Yet, for some reason, she found that she did not mention having just seen Demetrios.

"You might be right," the other girl answered, "although I'm not really caught up in that 'old memories' bit. I like this apartment. If there were a reason—a tall, dark, sexy reason—for staying in Greece I wouldn't mind keeping the place and sharing it with a new roommate."

Helen knew what, and who, she meant, but didn't encourage Lisa to continue. Their conversation quickly degenerated and Helen rose to leave. Somehow she felt uncomfortable in that glittering apartment making inconsequential conversation with Lisa.

"You're leaving already? It's early," Lisa protested.

"I promised Mrs. Caratides I would pick up some things for dinner on the way home. I really have to go," Helen fibbed.

"Come by tomorrow. We'll shop and then have a

sinfully extravagant lunch." Lisa really was desperate for company, Helen thought.

"Oh, I can't. Tomorrow's sightseeing day. I'm going out with Hercules and the Leighs." Well, that was true, even if not the complete story.

"And how is the handsome Hercules?" Somewhat regretfully, Lisa reminded her, "I saw him first, remember. I shouldn't have handed him over so easily; his replacement hasn't been all that cooperative. Want to change?"

When Hercules called for her the following morning his admiration was undisguised. Her sleeveless, scooped neck white dress showed off the dark glow of her suntan. Its pleated skirt swung gracefully against her long-legged stride.

"You are as brown as a gypsy, but much more lovely," he complimented her. "Athenian girls usually try to shield themselves from the sun."

"Well, I'm not an Athenian girl."

"Not yet," he said with a broad smile.

"Perhaps not ever," she countered tartly.

They found the Leighs alone. Helen didn't comment on Demetrios's absence until she saw them getting ready to leave. "But . . . I thought Dr. Criades was coming. Has he changed his mind?"

Allison looked at her closely. "No, he's going to meet us at the Acropolis." Helen met Allison's gaze and then looked down to hide any semblance of relief her eyes might reveal.

"Yes, that's the first stop, before it gets too hot," Jess said.

"The first?" Hercules groaned. "And how many stops are there to be? Isn't the Parthenon enough?"

"Young man, I don't think you appreciate your

country's ancient glory," Jess remonstrated jokingly.

"But I do," Hercules protested. "I just prefer to appreciate it sitting under an awning in a cool cafe and looking at the Acropolis from a pleasant distance, instead of climbing over those rocks with all the crowds of tourists."

"Well, I'm a tourist, and I want to see it up close. I want to see everything," Helen said, and Hercules groaned again.

Demetrios was waiting for them when they got to the Acropolis, but his back was turned and he didn't see them coming at first. His craggy profile was etched against the white marble beyond him and Helen caught her breath at the beauty of the scene against which he was silhouetted. He was standing before the Propylaea, a vestibule through which the Acropolis was entered.

"Good morning," Allison called, attracting his attention. "Hope you haven't been waiting long."

"It doesn't matter," he said, smiling his greeting to them. "One is never lonely here. My mind always journeys back in time and peoples this landscape with those who created it."

With Demetrios leading the way they walked through the two small temples, the Pinacotheca and the temple of the Winged Victory, as he narrated the history of the Acropolis. The Winged Victory commanded a superb view of the plains and the sea and islands of the Saronic Gulf, as well as the mountains of the Peloponnese beyond. It was breathtaking.

"I think this is my favorite view in the whole world," Allison said softly, moving close to Jess and taking his hand.

"I know," Jess responded. Helen envied them their closeness. Hercules had already moved away.

"Let's continue. The main attraction is the Parthenon," he called.

"He talks as if this were a performance," Demetrios said to Helen. "I'm afraid your young man is bored."

"He's not my—" Helen stopped. She didn't want to argue, not today, not here. "Well, I'm not bored. I've dreamed of this for years." Together they followed the other three back to the Propylaea.

"That's right. You were here once before, as a child."

"Yes," she said softly, "with my father. I had never seen him so moved."

"He was part Greek, wasn't he?"

"Yes, but that wasn't it. He felt the Hellenic heritage belonged to everyone. And here, it was in its most magnificent manifestation. . . ." Her voice trailed off as they passed through one of the gates to a rocky plateau. There it was, the western front of the Parthenon, its white columns of marble rising from the massive limestone base. It was staggering. She swallowed hard and just stared. She didn't realize she had stopped in her tracks until she felt Demetrios's hand on her elbow. Wonder and appreciation were in her eyes as she looked up at him.

His own gaze reflected the same, and something more. They moved on together, and when they reached the others, who had stopped to wait up ahead, Hercules eyed Demetrios coolly and, with a proprietary manner, took Helen's other hand. Demetrios moved away and resumed his narration.

The Sacred Way from the Propylaea to the Parthenon had once been lined with statues. The statue of Athena, the colossal achievement of the sculptor Phidias, had stood here.

"The plumes on her helmet and her raised spear could be seen gleaming in the sunlight by sailors approaching the coast," Demetrios said.

Helen looked up before her, the sun's rays in her eyes, and could almost visualize the ancient goddess outlined there.

"We have better means of navigation today, thank heavens," said Hercules as he took out a handkerchief to mop his brow. "It certainly is going to be hot today."

Irritated, Helen moved away to climb toward the Parthenon.

"The Virgin's Chamber," Demetrios, who was close behind her, explained. The exterior decorations had commemorated the history of Athena. All were the work of Phidias, and each was a masterpiece.

"Try to imagine a frieze over five hundred feet long and all brightly colored," Demetrios suggested.

"But it's beautiful with no decoration at all," Helen said breathlessly, knowing it was not the height which affected her. "There is such grandeur, such complete harmony. I can see why you come here so often."

"I do, but how did you know?"

"Oh, Alix mentioned it." Helen was embarrassed. She didn't want him to think she made a habit of discussing him with others. "She just mentioned that you said it . . . how did she put it?"

"Revives my spirit," he completed with a smile. "In a way it's my spiritual home."

"But you have another home, where your mother lives, I believe."

"Ah, yes. The home where I am refreshed in body."

"Well, that should take care of the complete man," she offered.

"Not quite. There is still the heart." She looked straight ahead, but she could feel his eyes on her face. "Have you forgotten the heart, Eleni?"

"It never ceases to amaze, does it?" Jess's voice came from close behind them and Helen turned to him in relief. She was still afraid to trust herself with Demetrios. He had been gentle, considerate and, yes, even romantic at Nauplion. But he could also be sarcastic and cold. Nor had she forgotten those other feelings which had almost caused her to lose her head that night in her room. Surrendering to those feelings had cost her her pride, if not her virginity. Would Demetrios have continued if Bertha hadn't interrupted? Remembering his harshness at the time, she wondered if his only motive had been to humiliate her.

Looking at him now, she saw a different person. He both absorbed and reflected the strength and beauty surrounding him. But the marble was inanimate, while he was vitally alive and interested as he continued his tour. Hercules, with his golden coloring and white uniform, repeated the hues and colors of the surroundings, but it was Demetrios who belonged there.

"Too bad you forgot your camera, Helen," Hercules remarked.

"I didn't forget it; I deliberately left it behind. You can lose the present moment by concentrating on capturing it for the future." Demetrios shot her a look of understanding.

"What's wrong with taking pictures?" Hercules asked, confused.

"Nothing," Helen said with a sigh. She relented and smiled at Hercules. He couldn't help being as he was. "There's plenty of time for pictures. I'll be returning often, I know."

"But now you have seen it. Will it be necessary for us to come back?" Again he mopped his brow and then added comically, "In the summer?"

"Not us, me!" Helen laughed.

"I think this visit will last Hercules another twenty years," Allison observed.

"At least until our children are old enough to be brought on a Sunday outing." Hercules didn't notice the looks the others exchanged or Demetrios's frown and blithely continued. "And then we will come in the autumn only."

Helen was furious. *"You* can come whenever you and your wife, whoever she may turn out to be, want to come. *I* am here now and I'm going to make the most of my visit." She got up and stalked away. Hercules gestured helplessly and followed her, but she shrugged him away when he tried to take her arm and he dropped back. Allison made a point of keeping him occupied while Demetrios caught up with Helen at the Erechtheium.

"You're disturbed," Demetrios commented.

"Hercules had no right to say that." Helen's voice trembled with anger.

"Apparently, he thinks he has." His tone was cold.

"I gave him no reason to assume anything," she insisted.

"I'm afraid you give conflicting messages, Helen. You don't seem to know your own mind."

"Of all people to talk about conflicting messages . . ." She turned her anger on him now. "You're the last person with the right to criticize."

"What do you mean?"

"Your split personality is what I mean. Or should I say personalities? It's ironic that you're a psychologist, because you seem able to change roles so easily. Pedant . . . student . . . critic . . . friend . . . seducer . . ."

"And lover. You forgot one," he added.

She was confused, hurt and angry all at once, and would have wanted to continue the conversation, but he gave her no opportunity. He resumed his description, but Helen couldn't summon the same interest as before. She only half heard the history of the graceful Erechtheum, with its legends of Poseidon and Athena. As she gazed at the caryatids, the six carved maidens supporting the roof of the elegant building, she envied them their complacent expressions. They seemed not to mind the burden they carried, while she felt the full weight of her emotional confusion, a less visible but still oppressive weight.

On their way down from the now crowded precipice they were besieged by photographers and vendors hawking souvenirs. Hercules, his spirits revived now that they were leaving, insisted that they have their pictures taken. He meant to be generous, insisting on treating them.

The photographer posed them for various shots. He took a group picture, then one of Jess and Allison, then one of the three others, then individual shots. Helen refused when Hercules wanted one of the two of them alone and he had sense enough not to persist. She relented a little as she watched him assume a pose for his own picture. He looked so boyish, so obviously pleased at being photographed.

Demetrios, by contrast, looked brooding. When they found a shady spot to sit and wait for the photographer to bring the pictures he allowed the conversation to eddy around him. Now that he was done lecturing he seemed to have little to say. Aware of the tension, Jess and Allison tried to revive the earlier enthusiasm of the group. Only Hercules seemed not to have lost his natural, if naive, good spirits. He was trying to entertain them with stories about some of the strange and funny tourists he had encountered on his cruises.

"Speaking of tourists," he suddenly remembered, "I almost forgot. Guess who I ran into last night in a cafe. Lisa, sitting by herself having a brandy."

"Didn't you just see Lisa yesterday?" Allison asked Helen.

"Yes, she said you two had visited earlier," Hercules eagerly continued, "and she knew about our sightseeing today. I think she is lonely, so I asked her to come along but, like me, she is not so much interested in ruins." His smile was ingenuous. "But I persuaded her to join us for dinner. I was sure you would not mind." He looked around.

Allison frowned slightly, but nodded.

"Sure, why not?" Jess agreed with his usual good nature.

Helen said nothing, concentrating on trying to fathom Demetrios's reaction to this bit of news, but his face remained impassive.

When the pictures were brought Hercules made a little production of giving them out. "So we will all have a memento of this day," he said, pleased with himself. Helen dropped hers into her bag without a word.

The rest of the day went as planned. A visit to the National Museum, a leisurely lunch, and then that treasure house of Byzantine art, The Benaki. Lunch somewhat restored Helen's vitality, but the closeness she had experienced earlier with Demetrios had vanished.

Hercules provided the afternoon's humor with his constant protestations that he had had enough culture that day to last him a lifetime. "No," he amended, "two lifetimes." But even his interest was aroused by the opulent collection of Greek national costumes displayed at the Benaki Museum.

"Look," he declared with awe, pointing to a sword with a richly jeweled hilt, "the sparkle from the stones would blind one's enemy and then one could pierce him easily." He made a lunging motion.

"I see that it's the bloodthirsty aspect of our history that excites you," Demetrios observed coolly.

"That's true," Hercules agreed, undismayed by Demetrios's disdain. "I like action."

"Which is why you're a seaman and Demetrios is a psychologist," Jess commented, stepping deftly between the two. "The man of action and the man of thought. And I, in the center, the perfect embodiment of both."

"I, unfortunately, am the perfect embodiment of the foot-weary wife of this perfect man," Allison said. "Enough for one day. I say let's find a nice café and enjoy a cool drink while we decide where to go for dinner."

"An absolutely perfect suggestion," Hercules seconded. "And since I told Lisa we would meet her at the Café Pano at six, let us go there."

When they reached Pano's Lisa had not yet arrived. The outdoor tables were crowded, mostly with American tourists. Still, Helen thought, it was nice to sit with an iced lemonade and watch the colorful parade of pedestrians, just as they watched the colorful array of patrons at the sidewalk café.

"Who's ogling whom?" she asked Allison with a laugh.

"Let's say it's reciprocal ogling," was Allison's amused reply.

"Talk about ogling, your young friend is going to get a lot of it tonight," Jess said as he watched the approach of Lisa Rhodes.

She was clad in a two piece knit outfit of electric blue with a skimpy chemise top which looked cool and was also quite revealing.

"Well, you must have had a full day sightseeing judging by how tired you all look," Lisa noted when she arrived.

And Helen felt that way—tired, dusty, and crumpled, in contrast to Lisa's crispness.

"And you?" Helen asked tartly. "Did you sleep all afternoon?"

"As a matter of fact, yes," Lisa answered. "Sightseeing's not my thing, as I mentioned yesterday, dear. But when Herc suggested dinner, that's another story, especially when he told me who would be here." She looked pointedly at Demetrios. "You didn't mention that Demetrios was going with you, Helen; I guess you forgot." The voice was sweet, but the implication wasn't.

Demetrios looked curiously at Helen, but she refused to meet his eyes.

There was a friendly argument about where to go for dinner. Demetrios suggested a quiet taverna, but Hercules opted for Aliki's, a chic club on the beach.

"They have entertainment and music," he coaxed. "We can dance."

"Oh, great." Lisa was enthusiastic.

"I thought you were tired from all the walking," Helen reminded Hercules.

"I have revived. Besides, we have not danced since the Olympia."

"It might be fun." Jess turned to his wife. "We haven't gone dancing in ages. We'll show these youngsters a thing or two."

"Sure we will," Allison smiled wearily, "if they play a slow waltz and if you hold me up." Jess laughingly agreed.

"I guess we're outvoted," Helen said to Demetrios.

"So we are," he agreed. "We'll have to make the best of it."

Apparently he wasn't going to have too much trouble making the best of it, Helen thought as she watched him go off to his car with Lisa clinging to his arm. She was quiet during the fifteen-minute drive to Aliki's, her thoughts turning to the conversation probably taking place in the other car.

Lisa was determined to be enchanting that evening. The liveliest of the group, she amused them with her chatter and her indefatigable zest. Whether Demetrios's response was just polite or reflected a real interest, Helen could not tell. She herself felt tired and had to force a gaiety she did not feel. Several times she felt Demetrios's eyes on her face, as if he was trying to read her thoughts. Deliberately, she forced herself to meet his glance with an assumed casualness and a smile.

Hercules had renewed his energy and wanted to dance every dance. When Helen insisted on stopping, he danced with Allison, and when he wore her out, Lisa was waiting.

The four at the table watched the dancers gyrating on the packed dance floor. "Where do they get their energy?" Allison asked enviously.

"I don't know," Jess replied. "They seem to refuel faster than we do. Maybe they're battery powered." The music changed to a slower number. "Come on," Jess said to his wife. "Here's that slow number you wanted. Maybe we can recharge your batteries?"

Allison looked at him fondly as she rose. "They need it, and you're the guy who can do it."

When they moved away, as if reading her thoughts, Demetrios said quietly, "They're good people. They're also very fortunate, are they not?"

"Yes." She sighed. She felt his gaze on her but this time she could not meet it and looked down. "You don't like this place, do you?" She looked up.

"No," he admitted. "It could easily be located in Los Angeles or in Nice. It has no special Greek character."

"And you prefer a Greek character?"

"I prefer a true character, Greek or otherwise." Abruptly, he stood up. "Come. I wish to dance."

She got up automatically; his tone allowed no refusal. As he steered her away she saw Hercules and Lisa coming back to the table. Was that why he had asked her to dance?

Demetrios held her lightly at first. He tried to guide her deftly in the crowd, but they were constantly jostled by the other dancers. His arms tightened around her and for an instant she stiffened, then softened against him. After all, it was just a dance. What could be the harm?

"Relax. It's been a tiring day. I'll hold you up as Jess does Allison," he said, lowering his chin against her hair.

"And recharge my batteries?" she asked, then instantly regretted the remark. She looked up to try to communicate to him the lightness of her intent, but his eyes were too close, too dark, too smoldering. Her quip died in her throat.

"And why not? People can draw strength from each other." His voice was low and he pulled her even closer.

"Please don't," she whispered.

"You're giving conflicting messages again, Eleni," he said. "Your words say one thing, but your body tells me a different story."

She knew he was right. Her rebellious body refused to heed her. It responded instead to the power of Demetrios, to the pressure of his lean strength against her. He let go of her hand and put both arms around her while her own arms crept up around his neck.

They moved sensuously to the music, though they seemed unaware of it. She wanted his closeness. She wanted more and she could not help herself. When the music ended she stood there; it was he who moved gently away.

"The musicians are taking a break. I'm afraid we'll be rather conspicuous if we keep standing here, much as we may wish to."

She tried to steady her voice as she said, "Saved by the bell, or by the end of the music, anyway."

133

He frowned. "Saved? What do you mean, saved?"

"Saved from myself, I guess. I can't blame you anymore. I don't seem to have any willpower when I'm with you. You proved that to me once already."

She started to walk away, but he pulled her back roughly. "Explain yourself," he ordered.

"That's just what I mean. You pull me to you and push me away at will. But you don't really care about me."

"You're a fool!"

"Perhaps I am. I should have more pride. But . . . but . . . all my resolve seems to disappear when you make love to me."

"I haven't made love to you yet. Not properly. When I do, you'll know it."

He sounded smug and she bridled. "Do you think you can just take me at will?" She struggled to free herself.

"Perhaps I can," he declared, "but I won't. I want to have you not by my will only, but by yours as well. No, if you come to me, it will be without the excuse, the solace, of helplessness. That is a defense mechanism I won't allow."

"You sound like a psychologist, not a lover."

"And you sound like a child, afraid to make a commitment. I want to help you to grow up."

"I'm not your patient."

His retort was stifled by Jess's approach. "Hey, you two, your coffee's getting cold. Finish the argument at the table and I'll referee, although you promised I wouldn't have to," Jess reproached Helen.

"You won't," she said. "The argument is over."

They rejoined the others, though Helen didn't

trust herself to speak at first. She was too near tears. When Hercules asked her what was wrong she snapped at him. Lisa looked appraisingly from Helen to Demetrios but made no comment. Diplomatically, Allison tried to revive the conversation.

"So many more tourists this year," she said, gesturing at the crowded dining room. "It's great for the economy, I'm sure, but it makes one want to get away from Athens."

"We'll get away. Just as soon as I finish up some things at school," Jess promised. He turned to Helen. "But you should make plans now, Helen. An island trip, perhaps. Or the monasteries at Meteora, the villages in the Peloponese. There are endless possibilities."

Hercules frowned. Obviously, he didn't approve. "But why leave Athens?"

Demetrios noticed his frown but ignored the question, saying to Helen, "You should go. There's much more to Greece than the cities."

"Didn't you say that your grandfather was Greek?" Jess recalled.

"Yes, my father's father."

"Do you know where he was from?" asked Allison.

"As a matter of fact, I do. It was a town named Limnaki."

"Limnaki?" Demetrios repeated, sounding surprised.

"Yes. My father used to talk about going there to see if any of his father's family remained. He never got the opportunity before he died. Do you know where it is?" she asked Demetrios.

"It's a village neighboring my own, only a few kilometers away. I know it well."

"Oh, Helen, what a coincidence! You should go." Allison was enthusiastic.

"Why don't we all go?" Lisa cried eagerly. "We'll plan an excursion. It would be fun."

Hercules disagreed. "Some of these little villages are very poor. Many do not even have paved streets. And they are very dull."

"There isn't much to do," Demetrios concurred. "I certainly wouldn't suggest a group excursion."

"But you go often," Lisa protested. "At least, that's what I'm told when I call you up. You're never available."

"Yes, I go often, but it's my home. I go to see my family and to . . ." he paused, searching for the right words, ". . . to be with people who still live simply, with basic values. They don't play games with each other as so-called sophisticated people do."

"But games can be fun, Demetrios." Lisa pouted prettily.

"They can also be dangerous," Demetrios responded, his tone ending the discussion. "It's late; let's go."

Helen expected that they would separate into the two cars as they had before, but Demetrios seemed to have different ideas. "Since your car is at the Leighs', Hercules, of course you will ride with them. And since your way home is closer to Lisa's apartment than mine, I'm sure you'll be happy to take her home. I'll drop Helen off at Mrs. Caratides's."

Without waiting for an answer, he took Helen's arm and steered her to his car. By the time Hercules managed to protest Demetrios had already started the engine.

Demetrios quickly drove off, leaving Helen completely subdued by his forcefulness.

They drove the whole distance without speaking, which made her wonder why he had been so set on driving her himself. When he pulled up in front of the darkened house he didn't turn the engine off. She was flustered. Did he just expect her to get out?

"I guess Bertha went to bed," she commented feebly. He said nothing.

"Thank you for taking me home," she went on. "Would . . . would you like to come up?"

He turned off the motor and looked at her searchingly. "Would *you* like me to come up?"

She didn't know what to say. "Well . . . I mean . . . since you made it a point to . . . to take me home . . . I thought you'd want . . ." She couldn't finish.

"I asked what *you* wanted." His voice was harsh. "Do you want me to come to your room? Do you want me to kiss you, to caress you, to undress you, to take you to bed?"

"Stop!"

"Do you want me to seduce you?" he went on relentlessly. "Apparently you see me in that role. Thank you, but I decline."

She felt as if she had been slapped. "Then why did you insist I come with you? Hercules wanted—"

He interrupted her. "Yes, let's talk about what Hercules wants. What role have you assigned him? Is he a seducer, also?"

"Of course not. He has honorable intentions." How awful and prim that sounded.

"Because he wants to marry you?"

"Yes."

"Is it honorable to marry a woman and insist on her dependence? Hercules expects a subservient wife."

"How do you know he's like that? He's kind and considerate."

"I know many young men like Phyllos. He is kind, yes. He means well, but he's limited and you know it. He has a certain boyish charm and he seeks a sweet wife with girlish charm, one who will never really grow up."

"You don't know that!"

"I can see it. And so could you, if you'd be honest with yourself. He would restrict you. He wants playfulness, not passion."

"And you?" The question came unbidden.

"I like the passion," he murmured, reaching for her. He kissed her slowly, deeply, his tongue parting her mouth and coaxing the response she knew she could not refuse. His hands were warm on her bare back. When he moved one hand to caress her breast she felt excitement surge within her.

"I said I wouldn't do this," he groaned against her lips. "I want the woman, not the girl."

"A woman like Chrysanthe? Like your wife?"

He pulled away, his face white and livid. "What are you saying? What do you know of Chrysanthe?"

She had touched a nerve. "I know you were married once. Apparently you've never gotten over it."

"You know nothing." He was bitter, but she noticed that he hadn't denied the marriage. "You're playing games again, assigning roles to people. This time you're giving me a past, a past based on gossip—a past to suit you."

Angrily, he led her from the car and walked her to

the front door. When he looked down at her, at her quivering mouth and confused expression, he relented a little. "Eleni, how old are you?" he asked gently.

"Twenty-six." Her voice quivered slightly.

"You are in Greece now. In the villages, girls mature . . . they become women . . . very early. You have some village blood in you. Give it a chance." He kissed her lightly on the cheek and left.

Chapter Eight

Hercules called the following morning, still angry at what he considered Demetrios's high-handed behavior. "Did he take you straight home?" he asked.

"Yes," she answered truthfully.

"Are you all right?"

"Yes." This time she lied.

Hercules went on. Did she remember that he would be going off with the ship for a few days? She did. Did she realize that he was leaving that afternoon? Yes. Could he stop by to see her? No.

"I have some work to do with Jess this morning. I'm sorry," she explained.

Hercules sounded disappointed, but accepted her excuse. "I shall call you the minute I return," he promised and hung up.

She felt spiritless and depressed. She had no work to do with Jess. Had she added lying to her habits?

She was glad Hercules would be gone. I guess I just don't know how to handle men, she thought. She needed some time to herself. When Allison called to invite her over, Helen put her off. She knew Allison was eager to talk about what had happened, but she didn't feel up to it. After all, she wasn't really sure what *had* happened.

She spent the morning in a futile attempt to concentrate on her Greek lessons. She sat in the garden, listlessly turning pages, but she knew her efforts were wasted. When Alexandra stopped by at noon Helen greeted the young girl eagerly.

"I missed you yesterday," Alexandra told her. "It was lonely with everyone away."

"We'll make up for it this week," Helen told her. "How about the beach today?"

Helen more than made up for the one day. Each day that week, they did something together. Was she trying to feel close to Demetrios through Alexandra? Helen asked herself. Did she hope to see him by being so often with the girl? She was getting to the point where she questioned everyone's motives, including her own. But, no, she assured herself. She really liked this child who was so affectionate and appreciative of their time together. Helen also recognized that she herself needed the undemanding and uncritical companionship; when she was alone, her confusion returned.

Hercules would return soon and again he would press his suit. She knew this and was irritated. Her thoughts, despite herself, turned to Demetrios. She tried to consider what he had said, to sort out his criticism. What did he expect from her? But invariably the memory of his physical presence would blur her reasoning as she relived his embraces, his kisses, his caresses.

Then, at the end of the week, she was on her way to the library to pick up Alix when she saw him. She stopped dead in her tracks. He was talking with

Alix, obviously delivering good news because the girl's face was alive with joy. When Alix spotted Helen she literally jumped up and down, her light hair flying silkily as she called, "Helen, Helen, we're going to the village."

Now that she had been seen, Helen had to join them. As she drew near Alix bounded over to her, grabbed her arm and pulled her jubilantly back to the serious-looking Demetrios.

"We're going to the village—tomorrow. It's a festival, St. Stephanos's feast day. It will be such fun!"

"I'm sure it will," Helen said fondly. Then she dared to look at the man. "How are you Demetrios?"

"All right." He did not look all right, she noticed; he looked tired.

"You look as though you could use a rest."

"It's been a busy week. I've resumed my practice, and I have some very difficult cases. And I have my hospital work. . . ." He shrugged. "There's always work."

"I missed you," Alix said.

"I missed you, too," he answered, but his eyes were not on Alexandra. "Thank you, Helen, for being so nice to Alexandra."

"I enjoyed her company," Helen assured him. "She kept me from being lonely as well."

"Oh, Demetrios, why cannot Helen come, too?" Alix suddenly asked. Then, charmed by her idea, she grasped his arm and again entreated, "Oh, please! How lovely it would be if she could come with us."

"Why . . . of course . . . if she would like," he said, caught by surprise.

What else could he say? Helen thought. Out loud, she demurred, "No, I really couldn't, but thank you."

"Oh, please, please," Alix begged. "There are farms and horses. *YiaYia* Criades cooks such wonderful things. And there's the festival, too." She enumerated all the temptations.

Demetrios spoke again, this time with a determination which sounded sincere. "Alexandra is right. There's ample room at my mother's house and you would enjoy the village. The celebration is an annual event, well worth seeing. Alexandra really wants you to come."

She wanted to ask, And what about you? but she didn't.

"Besides," he went on, "it will give you the opportunity to visit Limnaki."

Demetrios saw her hesitation and took advantage. "It's settled then. Alexandra, I'll pick you up here at eight and then we'll call for Helen. Have a pleasant afternoon; I shall see you tomorrow." He kissed Alix and then he was gone.

Late that afternoon Helen stopped by to see Allison, who she had been avoiding all week. Instead of asking questions, Allison simply made her a cup of tea and waited for Helen to initiate the conversation. Eventually, Helen did.

"I guess you're wondering what happened last Monday."

"Of course, I'm curious," Allison admitted. "I was rooting for Demetrios. The way he caught everyone off guard and just made off with you! It was beautiful. You should have seen Hercules's expression."

Helen had to smile. "Well, nothing happened. He

took me right home and we ended up fighting, as usual."

"Then why—?" Allison started to ask.

"I don't know why. Maybe he was trying to save me from Hercules, or Hercules from me."

Allison reached over and took her hand sympathetically and Helen's chin shot up. "It's O.K. I'm not going to let him bother me. I know I've said that before, but I mean it now. Apparently I'll have to become immune to him since I can't avoid him completely. As a matter of fact, I'm going to spend this weekend with him."

Allison stared in surprise.

"Oh, not that kind of weekend. Nothing romantic. It's the festival of St. Stephanos. He's taking Alexandra and she insisted that he invite me, so he couldn't say no."

"Are you so sure he wanted to?"

"Well, it wasn't his idea."

"Then why are you going?" Allison asked shrewdly.

"Because it will give me a chance to visit Limnaki. Kind of a pilgrimage to discover a part of my heritage."

"You know, Helen, if you really want to go to Limnaki without Demetrios Jess and I would be glad to take you."

Helen looked startled.

"But I think you want to go on this weekend." She saw that Helen was about to object but didn't allow her to interrupt. "And I think you should go. Get to know each other in a new environment; Demetrios may appear entirely different. That's his village—where he was born."

Helen recalled Allison's words the following day.

With Alix in the car, Demetrios had shown up right on time, but he looked his usual grim self.

At first they had little to say to each other. Demetrios concentrated on his driving, paying little attention to Helen or to Alix's constant chatter from the back seat.

However, as they left the urban area he slowly changed. The city faded behind them, the scenery became ruggedly beautiful, and Demetrios gradually threw off his grimness. He began to smile at Alix's exuberant comments, responding to her constant entreaties. Although he and Helen didn't converse much they were brought together by the girl's excitement.

Slowly he began to point out places of interest to Helen, glancing often in her direction. The closer they got to the village, the more relaxed he became.

"Are you sure your mother won't mind?" Helen asked. "Does she know she's having an extra guest?"

"Not yet." Demetrios was unperturbed. "But it will be fine," he reassured her. "Greek people take guests to their hearts. Even unexpected guests."

"I remember your lecture on the ship." How long ago that seemed to her. "What was it you described? *Philoxenia?*"

"Yes, a friendship towards strangers."

"But Helen and I . . . we're not strangers," Alexandra interrupted matter-of-factly. "We're practically family. Right, Demetrios?"

He hesitated only briefly; then he said, "Right, little one."

It was obvious that Alexandra felt like family. On arriving at the village she leaned out the window and called out to everyone she saw. People smiled and greeted her and waved to Demetrios, then looked curiously at Helen.

"You both seem to know everyone," she observed.

"That's not difficult. There are only five hundred people, more or less, in Agios Stephanos. Alexandra has come here often and has made many friends. And they'll all be at the *glendi* tonight."

"Glendi? What's that?"

Alexandra answered excitedly. "Oh, it will be so much fun. It will be in the square and there will be food and music and fireworks and dancing and ice cream and people from other villages and—" She seemed ready to go on and on.

"Don't raise Helen's expectations," Demetrios cautioned. "After Athens, she may be disappointed in our village entertainments."

"I'm sure I won't be," Helen murmured politely. Was he already sure that she wouldn't fit in?

Only the main street of the village was paved. Demetrios turned into one of the side streets, raising clouds of dust in his wake, and stopped in front of a stucco house, larger than those around it, with a long front veranda partially shaded by the second story overhang. It was filled with flower pots from which grew a number of different plants and herbs. They got out of the car and walked to the veranda, which felt cool and was redolent with the fragrance of the plantings.

"YiaYia," Alexandra called and flung herself into the arms of the woman who emerged.

"Doesn't *YiaYia* mean 'grandmother'?" Helen asked Demetrios in a whisper.

He looked at her curiously. "Yes," he said, making no effort to talk in a low voice. "Young people often call older women *'YiaYia'* as a sign of affection."

Unlike most of the country women Helen had noticed on their drive, this one was not dressed in black. She wore a simple blue cotton shirtwaist, its skirt partially covered with an embroidered white apron. Her black hair had been coiled, pulled back and pinned in a heavy bun. She moved with youthful ease, but Helen noticed gray at her temples and lines around her eyes. She had strong, handsome features; her eyes were piercing, dark and vibrant—Demetrios's eyes.

She was a tall woman, but he still had to stoop for her to cradle his face in her hands and then kiss both his cheeks.

"YiaYia, this is Helen, my friend." Alexandra made her introduction excitedly and impatiently. "Demetrios's friend, too. She's come for the festival. Now can I go find Loula, please?" Loula, she had told Helen, was her special friend in the village.

Mrs. Criades smiled indulgently. "Yes, Loula has been hoping you would come. But come home for lunch. Bring Loula," she called as Alexandra ran off.

Then Mrs. Criades turned her attention to Helen, who had been standing nervously in the background. Demetrios spoke a few rapid words in Greek to his mother then said in English, "Miss Stathos teaches at the American School, or will be teaching there this September. We persuaded her to come for the weekend."

"Of course. You are most welcome." Her voice was deep and she spoke English slowly. She took

Helen's hand as if to draw her into the family group. "Excuse my English. It is not so good now. I have had no practice for a long time."

"But you speak extremely well," Helen said sincerely and with some surprise. "Where did you learn the language?"

"My husband, Dimitri's father, went to university in New York City in America for one year. When I was a bride. He was all day in class, so I decided to study also. Today, it is more possible for girls to become educated. Those days, it was not considered proper."

"You could say my mother was a pioneer," Demetrios said playfully.

"Do not make fun, Dimitri," Mrs. Criades scolded. "You must not mind him, Miss Stathos. No, I shall call you Eleni, which we say in Greek, so you will feel at home. Dimitri teases too much."

"Yes, I'm well aware of that," Helen said dryly.

Mrs. Criades looked from Helen to her son and then back again. "So you know him well already. That is good. Then you know to pay little attention to his foolishness, as I do."

"Women!" He threw up his hands. "You stick together." But he was smiling.

"Why not?" His mother gestured him away. "Now, go take a walk, Dimitri. Go to the café to see your cousins. We will become acquainted."

Noticing Demetrios's look of suspicion, his mother declared, "Don't worry. We are not going to talk about you . . . too much. Go! Go!"

Somewhat reluctant, but smiling, he wandered off.

Within an hour Mrs. Criades had succeeded in

making Helen feel at home. She showed her the gardens, where she grew vegetables and lovingly tended her flowers. "One feeds the body, the other the soul," she commented. Then there was the barn where the two horses, "Alix's special favorites," were kept, and, of course, the chickens. Then there was the house itself, rustic but more than comfortable. How different from the Phyllos home, Helen thought.

The kitchen was very large, its wide-planked floor clovered with mats made of a heavy, burlap type fabric hand decorated with colorful floral designs. It was there that the two women eventually settled for their talk. Helen admired the house and commented on the modern kitchen and bath, unusual in the villages. Mrs. Criades gave Demetrios all the credit.

"Demetrios has done it all. Ten years ago we were very poor. As soon as he earned money, he began to fix the house."

"But if Mr. Criades was an educated man . . . ?" Helen questioned.

The older woman shook her head sadly and explained. Her husband had died when Demetrios was four years old. What money there was she had put aside for the boy's education while she lived frugally in the village.

"Today, it is different," she said. "Women work and can be independent. Like you. That is much better."

"You seem like a very independent woman to me," Helen said with sincerity.

"That is what Dimitri tells me. Especially when I disagree with him."

"I've noticed," was Helen's ironic comment.

"Perhaps he is spoiled, my son," Mrs. Criades said speculatively, "although not in the usual way. He had no brothers or sisters. He grew up very fast. In school, he had no rival. Always he was first. He is impatient sometimes, I know. It will be difficult for him to find a woman to please him, one who can understand the kind of man he is." Her look at Helen was penetrating and questioning.

"I hope you don't have the wrong impression." Helen was embarrassed by the unspoken question she sensed in Mrs. Criades's eyes. "We're not . . . I'm not . . . He doesn't even like me."

"You are mistaken," was the older woman's firm reply. "But perhaps you do not want to be. I should not like to see my son hurt. Beneath his growling he is . . . he can be . . . most tender, most loving."

Her words brought back Helen's memories of Nauplion and a gentle Demetrios walking with her on the *pareleia*. She would have liked to hear more but, at that moment, Alix and her friend Loula walked in with Demetrios right behind them.

Demetrios was positively jovial over lunch. He ate voraciously, accepted his mother's teasing about his huge appetite, observed that Helen's hearty appreciation of the meal should also be noted, and joked constantly with the two girls. Helen felt his eyes on her often during the meal and later when she helped clear up.

Afterwards they all rested for a while, the girls with Mrs. Criades in the large bedroom, Helen in the other bedroom, and Demetrios on a couch in the living room. Helen realized she had been given his bed. She tried to protest that she couldn't put him out of his room, but he cut her short.

"Don't be an idiot. Of course you will take the bedroom."

His mother's eyes signaled to Helen, advising acquiescence, as she explained. "Demetrios will be fine. He often sleeps on the couch, or even on a cot on the veranda when it is very hot."

In the bedroom, Helen took off her dress and lay on the bed in her panties and bra. The room was dim and peaceful, and she felt strangely at home. She slipped slowly into sleep.

Later, she didn't even hear the knock on her door. Alix finally opened the door impatiently. "Helen, get up. We're going to the vineyard."

Languidly, Helen stretched and looked up at the girl in the open doorway.

"Hurry, Helen. Demetrios is going to take us. In the wagon! Aren't you, Demetrios? The wagon, not the car."

"If you wish," a deep voice answered, and Helen realized with a start that he was behind Alix, peering over her head into the room. He was gazing at her half-clothed body as she lay in bed.

Alix ran off to go find Loula and Helen leaped out of bed to close the door. It resisted her push and, with dismay, she realized that he was holding it. She reddened with further embarrassment when he said, "Don't be so alarmed. As I remember, that yellow bathing suit was more revealing. Or do I offend your modesty?" Then he gently closed the door.

She dressed quickly, tying her hair back in a ponytail and putting on the straight-leg jeans and halter top she had worn on the ship, the outfit he had told her made her look like a little girl.

When she emerged Mrs. Criades nodded appreciatively. "It is nice that young women can dress thus today. Not so when I was young. Then, no trousers. No bare shoulders. Now it is much better."

"I agree," Demetrios concurred, his eyes slowly exploring Helen's figure.

Mrs. Criades could not be induced to join them. She had to finish her baking for the festival, she said. Helen offered to help, but she would have none of it. "I will accomplish more with all of you out of the way," she insisted.

Demetrios had hitched a horse to a cart which held the two girls in the back and the two adults on the driver's seat. The girls laughed excitedly as they drove off.

When they reached the vineyards Demetrios tethered the horse and they strolled through the rows of bright vines. "I've never seen seen so many grapes," Helen marveled. She had seen small arbors back home, but nothing like this lush growth. Alix took one of the bunches of still small and green grapes and popped one into her mouth. The others laughed when she made a face and spit out the sour pulp.

"It is not yet time. Grapes take time," Demetrios advised.

"But I thought you said things mature fast in the village," Helen commented softly, knowing she was misquoting him.

"Not the grapes, Eleni. I said the women ripen earlier." He looked around with satisfaction. "Perhaps it is the sun, the mountains, the earth, the air. Don't you feel the difference?"

She felt something, she knew. She felt a deep satisfaction and peculiarly at home.

"Yes, our girls ripen early," he said again, his eyes narrowing in a mocking appraisal of her. "There may be hope even for a transplant." He walked quickly back to the wagon.

They continued their tour, visiting a tobacco field and walking through an olive grove, then made their way slowly back.

Stopping at a café in the square for a cold drink, they watched the preparations underway for the festival. People were bringing in all sorts of things, tables and chairs and garlands and lanterns. A place was set aside for the musicians and another large space for the dancing. Women were beginning to bring some of the food, since each family contributed to the feast. In the back, pits had been prepared and the lambs were being turned on spits over the fires. Helen watched, fascinated by all the sights and sounds and smells.

"Do the women get dressed up for the party?" Helen asked. "Should I change?"

He looked her over carefully, his eyes amused again as he answered. "That's up to you. Do you want to attend as a little girl . . . or as a woman?" She blushed.

Mrs. Criades was more helpful. "Oh, do not dress up as in the city, but a dress or a skirt would be best."

There were a dozen trays of baked goods in the kitchen, *baklava, kourabiedes, fineekia*. Helen looked from them to Mrs. Criades and said admiringly, "How do you do it? You've been baking all afternoon and still manage to look beautiful and not the least bit tired. You're remarkable."

Mrs. Criades acknowledged the compliment with a smile, then said to her son, "Demetrios, I am glad you have found a young woman of such intelligence. She has excellent taste—except in men." Laughingly, she ordered, "Go now, all of you. Get ready. Demetrios, before you dress you must take the trays down to the square. Helen can shower first."

"Mama, you should have been a general," he said and complied.

Helen, too, did as she was told. It was not difficult to choose what to wear since she hadn't packed an extensive wardrobe for the weekend. Fortunately, she had brought a flared white skirt with a green, leafy pattern. She put on a white T-shirt with a light green binding on the sleeves and around the wide V neckline. It molded her body, outlining the swelling curves of her breasts, as revealing as the halter, but in a different way. She brushed her dark hair, leaving it loose on her shoulders. A touch of powder, light pink color on her lips and she was ready.

When Demetrios saw her he said, "I see you chose the dress. I'm glad." He had changed from his dusty denim pants and wore blue slacks and a white, buttonless shirt, loose and blouselike. He looked quite romantic, she thought.

"Why do you look at me so?" he asked.

"You look . . . different."

"You mean like a peasant?" He flashed a smile.

"More like a pirate," she corrected, "but certainly not like a proper and pompous psychologist."

He laughed. "Good! Tonight I shall be a pirate; I leave behind my pomposity."

Helen smiled and walked outside, where the others waited.

"But I warn you, Eleni, I also leave behind my propriety." His voice softly followed, sending a shiver through her.

The square was filled with villagers; Alix ran off to join Loula where all the young people had congregated. Mrs. Criades, Demetrios and Helen made their way through the people, with frequent stops for greetings and introductions, to a table near the music and dance area. Not trusting her Greek vocabulary yet, Helen acknowledged all introductions with a smile and "Hello." She was always given a warm smile and sometimes a vigorous handshake.

"I see what you meant by *philoxenia*," she said to Demetrios.

"They're pleased that you have come to our festival," Mrs. Criades noted.

"I'm sure all your guests are made to feel welcome, festival or not," Helen told her.

"Demetrios does not bring guests, except for Alix," his mother offered. "Not for a long time have we had a young woman in his bedroom."

When was the last time? Helen wondered. When he had brought home a rich young wife years ago?

"Mama," Demetrios laughed, "you make it sound risqué, even illicit. But then, why not, since tonight we're abandoning propriety, eh, Helen?"

She didn't know whether to agree or not. In this mood, Demetrios was hard to resist, but she had been hurt before when she had lowered her guard. Still, the atmosphere tonight was conducive to gaiety, so she decided just to enjoy the evening.

The meal was delicious, and Helen tasted so many Greek delicacies that she couldn't even begin to remember all the names. Then came the dancing. The villagers, both men and women, were dancing in several circling lines, holding their joined hands aloft as they performed the intricate steps. The leader, who held a white handkerchief, set the pace.

"Look!" Helen pointed. One young man was kneeling and bending backward until his head touched the ground behind him, responding to the yelled encouragements of the other dancers. "Bravo, Manoli," they shouted, and Helen, too, called out, "Bravo! Bravo!" Demetrios and Mrs. Criades laughed at her enthusiasm.

"Would you like to join a line?" Mrs. Criades asked.

Helen drew back. "I couldn't; I don't know how."

"It is not difficult. When they play something slower, I shall show you," the older woman promised.

A group of men had congregated around the table where the wine was being served. "Dimitri," they called. He excused himself to join them, and was greeted with good-natured laughter. Helen watched covertly as they talked. They all seemed at ease together. Demetrios, however, stood out, not as an outsider, Helen thought, but as a leader. His head was higher, his smile wider, his tone lustier.

She looked away and tried to concentrate on the dancers. They were so vigorous and joyful. She watched an old woman—she must have been almost eighty—being pulled to her feet by a clamoring family group. Finally, with a resigned smile, the woman took the handkerchief and began to dance. Her right hand on her hip, she moved lightly through the familiar steps. Amid cries of *"Yassou, YiaYia"* she led her group through the other dancers.

When the pace quickened most of the dancers retreated, mopping their brows in the warm night. "This is the Sailors' Dance, traditionally for the men," Mrs. Criades informed Helen.

The flickering lanterns cast the only light as a group of seven men moved forward. Their arms lay across each other's shoulders as they started to move in the rhythm of the dance. They were of different ages and sizes but moved in a single sinuous rhythm, leaving Helen fascinated. She had seen the young sailors dance together on the ship, but there had been an artificial, nightclub atmosphere to their performance. This was different.

She heard the leader call gruffly, "Come," as he drew another figure from the shadows to the head of the line. The newcomer moved easily into the dance, his body supple and strong, at one with the music. The dance required strength as well as grace, Helen realized, as she watched him leap, turn, kneel and leap again. The crouching was accompanied by a hitting of the ground, as if the touch renewed contact between the man and the earth. Was this a mystical ritual and the dancer a young god from Greece's Golden Age? But there was gaiety in the dancer, too, like a shepherd, dancing joyfully after coming down from the mountain. Suddenly he turned and his face was exposed in the light of the lantern. Helen's breath caught in her throat. It was Demetrios.

But what a Demetrios! So different from the critic at the interview in New York! So different from the formal man on the Olympia. So different from the impatient and judgmental analyst in Athens.

Helen looked at Mrs. Criades. The woman gazed at her son with deep love and the suggestion of tears. Impulsively, Helen reached over and squeezed her hand.

"His father danced like that, too," Mrs. Criades said huskily. "He could dance as if he forgot the world."

157

The music changed to an old folk song; it was greeted with enthusiasm as family groups again rose to dance.

"Come," Mrs. Criades insisted. "This is an old one and very easy to learn." Feeling self-conscious, Helen allowed herself to be led into a line of dancers. Mrs. Criades instructed her at first, then Helen simply watched the dancers' feet and followed the pattern. She soon got the rhythm, if not the exact steps, and began to enjoy herself.

"Good," Mrs. Criades complimented her and the other dancers smiled their encouragement.

"Bravo, *Americana,*" an old man called from the sidelines with such evident good will that Helen lost all her self-consciousness. Someone broke into the line next to her and took her hand, holding it very tightly. Even without looking, she knew it was Demetrios. His touch had become familiar, as had the excitement which it aroused.

They danced and danced, her full skirt swirling around her long legs. The leader called to Demetrios to take the first position. He did, pulling her with him. She took the end of the handkerchief and danced beside him. His eyes were on her constantly, commanding her to follow his lead. Winding through the other groups of dancers, he led his line to the outer edge of the square. There, suddenly, he handed the handkerchief to the man on the other side of Helen, took her hand and pulled her out into the surrounding darkness.

She had no chance to protest, nor any desire to do so. They walked some distance away to a patch of garden and trees. The air there was cooler and had a fresh, tangy scent. Helen inhaled deeply.

"Lemon trees," Demetrios identified them.

"It's almost intoxicating," she whispered.

"Yes," he said, as his arms encircled her. Her hands wound around his neck and she raised her mouth for his kiss. She felt the same surge of hunger she had experienced before, but did not try to subdue it. She let her fingers caress his hair and passionately returned his kiss. Tonight was different. The warmth of the festival, the magic ritual of the dance, and the wildness of their kiss were part of the enchantment. Let the problems and confusion return tomorrow. For now, they did not exist for her.

His kiss deepened and she felt a tremor go through him.

"What are you doing to me?" he muttered.

Her voice was breathless. "And you to me?"

"I know what I want to do, right here and now in this lemon-scented grove. I know what I want to do to you." His lips caressed her face. "I want to know you completely. I want to have you completely."

"Yes," she breathed.

"Is it the girl or the woman who says yes?" he asked softly.

She didn't know. She didn't want to answer questions. Tonight was to be ruled by magic, not reason.

But he would not have it so. He moved away. "I'm being unfair. This isn't the time." He took her hand to lead her back to the square.

Alix was sitting sleepily at the table where Mrs. Criades was gathering things together. The crowd was thinning out.

"Come, my children," Mrs. Criades greeted them. "It has been a long day." She looked from one to the other. "But, I think, a very good one."

Chapter Nine

In her room that night Helen tried to sort out all the emotions the day had brought. Allison had been right. In this environment, Demetrios was different. Helen had been allowed to see the Demetrios Alix knew and she could easily understand why the girl loved him so. What would happen tomorrow? she wondered. Would the old Demetrios return?

She undressed and started to put on her night-gown, then discarded it; it was too hot. She lay down, acutely aware that she was in Demetrios's bed, a thought both disturbing and strangely comforting. She pulled the single sheet over her and slept.

When she awakened Sunday morning she was disoriented. The sun was in her eyes and felt warm on her body where she had pushed the sheet down to her waist as she slept. She realized where she was and a small sleepy smile curved her mouth. She heard a sound and looked toward the door, which was halfway open. Demetrios, bare chested, his hand still on the doorknob, stood in the opening, more in than out of the room. His rapt look changed when he saw her startled embarrassment. As she pulled the sheet up to her chin, a smile came to his lips.

Quietly, he stepped inside. "I didn't mean to disturb you. I wanted to come in quietly to take a clean shirt from my bureau here, but I was distracted from my mission. The vision of the lovely young lady sleeping nude in my bed was most distracting . . . and tempting."

"Demetrios, if you . . ."

"After all, it *is* my bed." He grinned. "Each day quite literally I see more of you. Too bad we won't be here tomorrow." When he saw that she was about to speak, he cautioned, "Don't talk too loudly or we'll be discovered. You, still rosy with sleep, naked in bed. And me, with only my trousers on, here in the room with you."

"But you just came in," she pointed out.

"Ah, but who would know that?" he asked with feigned seriousness. His voice became insinuating. "I would be assigned the guilt without having had the joy of the experience. And as for you, your virtue would be compromised."

"And what would that mean?"

With a more serious expression, he looked at her. His eyes had a tender glow, or was it only the sun shining in hers?

"More than I think you're prepared for." Demetrios seemed to sigh, then said in a cheerfully pragmatic way, "And since the thought of you in my bed like this is most disquieting, I shall give you only five minutes to get up and come to breakfast."

He turned away, pulled out a bureau drawer, removed a shirt and opened the door to leave. When he was halfway out the door, he turned and threatened, "Or I'll come back and drag you out of bed." He disappeared.

The others were already at the breakfast table outside on the veranda when she appeared, dressed in her halter and jeans of the day before.

"Good, you are up. The day is too nice to lose," Mrs. Criades commented. Helen smiled her agreement, then wrinkled her nose slightly at the hot milk Mrs. Criades was pouring for her.

The older woman laughed. "I know that hot milk is not an American custom. I have strong Greek coffee ready, as well."

Helen compromised by pouring some of the coffee into the milk and found it had a pleasant, rich taste. They had hard-crusted bread sprinkled with sesame seeds, and scrambled eggs.

"Fresh," Alix announced. "I myself stole them from the chickens this morning."

"Well, you can atone for your theft in church this morning, little one," Demetrios said fondly. "Helen and I are driving to Limnaki, where her grandfather was born."

"But why not wait until church is over so we can all go?" Helen suggested.

"No, I must help the women clean up after the *glendi*," Mrs. Criades said. "There is much to do. And I'm sure Alexandra wishes to spend the day with Loula." She was decisive, her tone not allowing for argument. But then, Helen didn't really want to argue. Soon she and Demetrios were on their way, alone.

When they reached Limnaki the bells were ringing and people were walking to the church which dominated one side of the square. It was a little smaller than the church in St. Stephanos, but very picturesque. It was enclosed in a low-walled garden area, its white Byzantine dome gleaming in the sun.

Demetrios parked the car so they could walk around. Helen noticed that only the women and children seemed to be going into the church; most of the men had congregated outside in small groups, smoking and talking.

"How odd," she said to Demetrios.

He didn't think it odd at all. "That is customary. The men put on their church-going clothes and, in fact, they actually do go *to* the church, but not inside. The boys go as children," Demetrios went on, "and they'll attend again when they grow old. For now, the men use the time to solve the problems of the world or, at least, the village. More policy is made, more arguments settled, and sometimes started, outside church on Sunday than in the government offices."

They went on to take a leisurely walk through the town, a town in many ways similar to St. Stephanos, even to the unpaved side streets. When she tripped on a rock Demetrios took her elbow and then continued to hold her arm as they walked. She liked the feeling and smiled to herself.

The streets were quiet, since most people were at church. Helen looked around with a strange curiosity. This was where her grandfather had been born; one of these houses could have been his home before he left to start his new life in America.

As if he had read her thoughts, Demetrios mused, "I wonder which of these was your grandfather's house. Imagine, had he not emigrated, you might have been born right here in Limnaki." Suddenly he laughed. "We might even have met as children."

After a while, they found themselves back in the village square. Since it was Sunday, the little shops lining the square were closed, but Helen looked into windows and read the signs which announced their profession: Papadoulis—Carpenter; Kariotis—Tailor; Elefterios—Mechanic. . . . Demetrios helped her translate and then pointed out a sign, larger than the others, above the one open establishment, the café. It read STATHOS—CAFFENEION.

"There, Eleni! See, the Stathos family is still here in Limnaki."

"They couldn't possibly be the same family," she said doubtfully.

"Of course they're the same family. In a village, everyone is related. What was your grandfather's first name?"

"Aristedes, Aristedes Stathos."

They sat at one of the small outdoor tables and a stocky, middle-aged man with a thick head of dark hair and a luxurious moustache came to take their order. Demetrios ordered coffee and, when the man brought the steaming sweet brew, started a conversation with him.

They spoke so quickly that Helen couldn't follow, but she heard the name "Stathos," then "Aristedes Stathos." Demetrios gestured towards Helen. "Eleni Stathos," he told the man and the proprietor became excited.

"Manolis Stathos," he announced. With a happy cry, he leaned over to embrace Helen and to kiss her on each cheek.

Laughing at her startled look, Demetrios explained. "He's your cousin. His grandfather was the brother of Aristedes Stathos who went to the United States. He says you're family."

She wasn't sure what that meant. What was she supposed to do? The evident pleasure in Manolis Stathos's face brought a smile to her own. Encouraged, and waving his arms excitedly, he let loose a volume of words.

"Wait! Wait!" she said, laughing. "Slow down. I don't understand."

"He's so happy to have found his American cousin that he wants us to go to his house. He says you must meet his wife Sophia and his children, seven of them. He's invited us to dinner." As Demetrios translated, Manolis nodded happily.

"Oh, no, we can't. We're leaving for Athens this afternoon; we have to get back to Agios Stephanos," Helen tried to explain. She repeated her excuses using whatever Greek words she knew.

Manolis's expression saddened. Then he spoke quickly again, asking Demetrios to translate.

"Manolis is disappointed, but insists you must come again. Next time, not to St. Stephanos, but here to Limnaki, to your own village, to your own relatives. When you come, he will invite all the Stathoses living in the village for a big celebration."

Overcome by his enthusiasm, Helen just smiled and said, "Maybe, maybe another time."

Manolis must have assumed she had agreed as he looked quite happy again. He sat with them while they finished their coffee and, when church services were over and the villagers streamed away from the church, Manolis called to his friends and proudly pointed out his American cousin.

Helen became uncomfortable. "I think we should be going," she whispered to Demetrios. He looked at her curiously and she sensed his displeasure, but he rose to go. After an affectionate goodbye from Manolis, they returned to the car.

Demetrios was quiet on their return trip. Helen, too, was busy with her own thoughts. The immediate intimacy offered by Manolis Stathos had confused her. Although he had never seen her before he had accepted her at once as family. She was both pleased and disturbed by this; it was so different from the upstate New York reserve to which she was accustomed.

Finally, when they were almost home, Demetrios spoke. "Will you go to visit?" he asked.

"I don't know, Demetrios." She voiced her confusion. "He said it was my village, but I'm a stranger there. And relatives . . . people I don't know. I'd be embarrassed."

His voice sounded cold. "Because they're not rich or well-educated?"

She was hurt. "Of course not. I'm not that kind of a snob."

He was unconvinced. "I'm sorry, Helen, but you shouldn't have promised if you didn't mean it. Manolis will be very hurt now if you don't go back."

"But I didn't really promise."

"That was how it was interpreted. You could see that."

"I just didn't know how to handle him. I wasn't prepared. I thought we were just going to drive around for a while and then leave."

"Like a tourist." His voice was sharp. "Just a fast sightseeing tour, then goodbye. No commitment."

"You just don't understand."

"I'm afraid I do. You look on us as quaint, a

charming part of the Greek experience, but something to be taken only in small doses from a distance. A close connection is distasteful."

"That's not true. And you say 'us' as if you haven't also removed yourself from this life."

"Not removed," he corrected. "Never removed. Agios Stephanos is where I was born and brought up. It will always be a part of my life."

"But I notice that you took advantage of the chance to marry a rich girl years ago. Too bad it didn't work out."

"What does that have to do with this?" He was coldly furious. "You think I married for riches . . . to get out of the village?"

"Well, why did you marry?" How she wanted to know the answer to that!

"It has nothing to do with you."

She wanted to cry out, "But it does. It has everything to do with me. Did you love Chrysanthe Likakes? Do you love her still?" But she said nothing and they finished the ride in silence, just as they had begun.

When they arrived in Agios Stephanos there was another car parked in front of the Criades house. With a sinking sensation Helen recognized it as Hercules's car. He was sitting with Mrs. Criades on the veranda. When Demetrios saw him, he stiffened and stopped short, taking Helen's elbow to stop her.

"I see you have arranged to have your boyfriend come to pick you up." He looked livid.

"But I didn't know . . ." She tried to explain that Hercules's presence was a surprise to her, but Demetrios wasn't listening.

"What's the matter? Did you feel that a full two

days would be too much to spend with me in the village? Or were you afraid you would miss your young man?"

"He's not my young man," she pleaded, but his eyes were still narrowed in anger. She gave up. "Apparently you've made up your mind what to think, so it's useless for me to explain." She pulled away from him and moved to the veranda.

Hercules did not let her cool greeting dampen his good spirits. "When Mrs. Caratides told me you had come to St. Stephanos for the festival I decided to drive down to surprise you," he announced. That his surprise had not given any of the three listeners much pleasure did not occur to him.

His statement did, however, make Demetrios aware that he had been wrong, that Helen had not known of Hercules's intent. Demetrios turned to her. "I was wrong; I'm sorry." But his voice carried no emotion.

"Don't apologize." Her tone was icy. "I'm sure you'll be relieved not to have to put up with me on the return trip."

Mrs. Criades gazed sadly from her son to Helen, then back again, but she remained silent.

"I'll get my things, Hercules," Helen said. "I'll be ready in a few minutes."

Hercules was completely confused by what was going on. "But we do not have to leave right away. It is still quite—"

"We may as well," she interrupted. "As long as you took it upon yourself to come, I'd just as soon leave now." She stalked off to gather her things.

When she said goodbye a few minutes later Demetrios's face was white under his tan. His eyes, which could glow with amber light, were dark, fathomless. She felt that if she looked deeply into them she would be swallowed.

"Tell Alix I'll see her soon, maybe tomorrow," she told him.

"So you *can* think of someone else," he said with tight sarcasm.

Think of someone else? Her whole being cried out silently for him! These two days had been so happy. Why did they have to end like this? But she said nothing, keeping her face as impassive as his.

She hugged Mrs. Criades and thanked her.

"So, you go," the older woman said. "But come back to us, Eleni, perhaps when you both are wiser." With resigned disapproval, she looked at Helen and her son.

When they arrived at Mrs. Caratides's house Hercules wanted to stay, but Helen insisted that she was tired. She twisted away when he tried to kiss her, then darted inside.

Tomorrow she would tell Hercules that she couldn't see him anymore. There was no reason to encourage him to think that their relationship would lead to marriage. He actually expected it to happen, given time. But she didn't really feel sorry for him; she knew that it was his pride, more than his heart, which would suffer.

As she started upstairs she heard Bertha calling to her from the kitchen. She couldn't ignore the old woman, although she didn't feel like talking. Bertha poured coffee, and they sat companionably, sipping their coffee while Bertha waited for Helen to say something about her trip.

Finally, unable to contain her curiosity, Bertha asked, "Agios Stephanos—the *glendi* was nice?"

"Oh, yes. Very nice," Helen replied, with deliberate brevity.

Bertha continued, "You like Kyria Criades?"

"Yes, very much. She is a fine woman."

"Widow, like me," Mrs. Caratides noted. "I have one child. She have one. He is good son?"

"I don't know. I suppose so." Helen didn't want to discuss Demetrios. She finished the coffee, careful not to drink the grounds which filled the bottom of the cup. She started to get up when Bertha, looking at her shrewdly and sensing that something was wrong, stopped her.

"Wait! I read."

Helen didn't know what she meant.

"I read coffee."

Bertha reached over and tipped Helen's cup upside down on the saucer. Intrigued, Helen sat down again. "I've heard of reading tea leaves, but never coffee."

Bertha waited a few more seconds for the grounds to drain down, then lifted the cup to reveal a dark design that the grounds had formed on the saucer. Bertha picked it up and studied it closely. Finally, she pointed. "Is you," she said, "by yourself," indicating a small design apart from the rest. "Here," Bertha's finger moved towards the larger pattern, "Here is man, dark man."

"Oh, Bertha! The whole blob is dark. How do you know it is a dark man?"

"I know. Dark man," Bertha said firmly. "And here is child."

"Alexandra, his child," Helen said, not realizing

she had given away where her thoughts were. Demetrios was her "dark man."

"No," Bertha disagreed. "Small child. Maybe your child." Her finger traced another design and shaped a structure with a dome. "A church. A Greek church." Bertha put the cup down. "You marry dark man in Greek church and have nice baby," she concluded complacently.

How Helen longed to believe that prediction. She sighed as she remembered the way she had parted from Demetrios earlier. "I'm afraid not, Bertha. This weekend was a mistake. Perhaps this whole trip was a mistake." She got up wearily. "I'm tired. I think I'll lie down for a while."

Her depression lasted through the next morning. Perhaps she should never have left home. She had wanted a change from the routine of South Elmsford; she had hoped for new challenges, perhaps a romance, not confusion and grief. When Allison called to invite her to lunch, she accepted gratefully. She wanted to talk to someone.

Allison greeted her at the door. "I can't wait to hear about your weekend." They sat in the living room. A close scrutiny of Helen's face told Allison something was amiss. "Uh, oh! Something tells me it didn't go right. What happened?"

"The same old story when it comes to Dr. Demetrios Criades and me," Helen replied bitterly. "Always an unhappy ending." She ran through events of the weekend. "It had all been so great, but it ended so badly," she said, near tears. "We had never felt so close before. I even slept in his bed," she added childishly, the memory making her heart race.

"You're in love with Demetrios." Allison guessed the truth.

"No, I won't allow myself to be."

"I've suspected it for a long time. Helen, admit it."

"Why? So I can be hurt some more?" Talking had only made her feel worse. Despite Allison's attempts to persuade her to stay, Helen found an excuse to leave.

"I told Alix I would see her at school today." That was partly true, but the real reason was she didn't want to hear Allison continue in the same vein.

"But we haven't had lunch," Allison protested.

"I'm not hungry. I'll get something later." Helen darted out.

Why not go to see Alix? She didn't want to return to her room. Alix might have been upset by her abrupt departure from St. Stephanos yesterday, and she had told Demetrios to tell the girl she would see her at school.

She walked alone for a while, wandering aimlessly on the deserted school grounds, Allison's words repeating in her head: "You're in love with Demetrios."

Once she had told herself that she wouldn't allow herself to love him. It was too late for that. Allison was right. There was no longer any question of *allowing* herself; she had no choice. She loved Demetrios Criades, loved him desperately, completely, and permanently. Nothing would come of it; nothing could come of it, but she could no longer deny her emotions.

Her grief was no less, but she felt strangely relieved. She had accepted this truth. Was that what

Demetrios would describe as behaving like a woman? But what did it matter now?

Helen found herself on the path to the school library. Outside the building she saw Alexandra with an older, very elegant, gray-haired woman.

Alix greeted Helen eagerly. "Demetrios said you might stop by. I hoped you would come in time to meet grandmama." She introduced Helen to Mrs. Likakes.

"Helen is my best friend," she told her grandmother proudly.

"Thank you. But, of course, you also have Demetrios," Helen reminded Alix. Her eyes, however, were on the older woman as she looked for some reaction to the name. There was none, just a friendly smile.

"We're going to Cannes tomorrow, Helen. Grandmama and I." Alix was bubbling over. "We're going on vacation. There'll be swimming and a boat and . . . Oh." She stopped suddenly, then said, "I wish you could come, too. I'll miss you." But the girl could not sustain any interruption of her joy. "But I'll see you in September. And you'll have Demetrios." Innocently, she flashed a smile and ran off to get her things.

Helen winced inwardly.

"I so appreciate your friendship to my granddaughter," Mrs. Likakes said. Helen studied the woman's face, heart-shaped, with small, delicate features and still very attractive. She must have been very beautiful. Had her daughter resembled her?

"Being friends with Alexandra is a pleasure," Helen assured Mrs. Likakes. "I enjoy her company."

"You're too kind. I had to be away for a long period this time; I know she was lonely before you came."

"But Demetrios is always attentive," Helen heard herself say. "Demetrios is always there, isn't he?" Why was she bringing up his name like this? She was deliberately wounding herself, but she couldn't help it.

The other woman eyed her curiously. "Yes . . ." she drawled slowly, "Demetrios has been a good friend to Alix, and to my family."

"Surely more than a friend," Helen persisted. "After all, he was part of the family for a while—I mean . . . I've heard that . . . he and your daughter . . ." Helen paused, feeling stupid. Why had she started this? What did she hope to gain except the older woman's resentment of her rudeness.

But there was no resentment in the eyes which scrutinized her so sympathetically. Mrs. Likakes seemed to see behind Helen's clumsy attempt to question her on Demetrios's connection to the Likakes family. "Alexandra has told me that you and Demetrios are . . ." she paused delicately, ". . . close friends. Perhaps more?" she suggested.

"No, not more," Helen denied. "Demetrios will never allow anyone to replace your daughter."

"Ah, I see." Mrs. Likakes sighed gently. "The old rumors persist. Demetrios chooses to ignore them. In his pride, he insists on letting people say what they will, believe what they wish. But I think, with you, the truth is necessary."

She drew Helen firmly into the cool anteroom of

the library. Sitting down on the marble steps, she motioned to Helen to sit beside her.

"I think, my dear, you should know what really happened between Chrysanthe and Demetrios. I sense that you have a mistaken assumption, one which is hurting you both."

Slowly, sadly, Mrs. Likakes proceeded to relate to Helen what had happened over twelve years ago. The story was not what Helen had expected.

Demetrios and Chrysanthe Likakes had been friends at college, good friends, but nothing more. She hadn't been a good student and Demetrios had spent a lot of time tutoring her; he had been like a brother.

"Chrysanthe was not stupid," Mrs. Likakes explained, "but immature and frivolous. Tragically so, as it turned out." Chrysanthe had fallen in love with a young Frenchman who had abandoned her when she became pregnant. She had wanted to die and had even attempted suicide by cutting her wrists. It was Demetrios who had found her and saved her life. After that, she had become terrified of her father and of what he would do if he found out. She begged Demetrios to help her.

"You mean . . ." Helen was beginning to see the truth.

"Yes," Mrs. Likakes answered the unspoken question. "Demetrios married Chrysanthe because, having saved her once, he now felt responsible for her. He was afraid she might try to harm herself again if her father discovered her dishonor." So Demetrios had assumed the burden of her father's anger. The rest of the story was as rumored, the annulment, Chrysanthe's removal to Switzerland, the birth of Alexandra, Chrysanthe's accidental death two years later.

So Demetrios was not Alix's father after all, Helen realized. He had married the unfortunate Chrysanthe to save her. But had he also loved her? Helen wondered if she would ever know the answer to that question.

Chapter Ten

What now? Helen wondered as she left the campus. Hercules was definitely out of her life. She couldn't marry him and would tell him so at the first opportunity. Alix, her gay little companion of recent weeks, was also gone. And she had despaired of seeing Demetrios again until business brought them together.

Why should he want to see her? He thought her a snob, both childish and selfish. He had no idea what she was really like. Couldn't he see how much she cared for him?

Then Helen reminded herself that she, too, had refused to recognize how she felt. How could she expect him to see a truth that even she had not acknowledged? But he was a psychologist, she reasoned defensively; he was supposed to be able to fathom how people really felt.

She decided to return to Allison's. She owed her friend an explanation.

"You were right, Allison," Helen confessed when

177

they were again sitting together. "I *am* in love with Demetrios Criades. You knew it before I did, or at any rate before I was willing to admit it."

"Well, it's about time you came to your senses." Allison was triumphant. "But why so sad? Love is wonderful. Look at me and Jess. Or better not look at me and Jess! We hardly personify romance at its height. Think of Romeo and Juliet."

"They didn't exactly turn out well," Helen pointed out.

Serious now, Allison said gently, "Then *do* look at me and Jess. I joke about it because I'm a little afraid of admitting how lucky we are. After seven years, Jess and I love each other more than ever. That's what I want for you."

"I want it, too," Helen cried. "Closeness and understanding as well as desire. But that's impossible for me."

"Why?" Allison wanted to know. "If you love each other . . ."

"Each other? That's just it!" Helen exclaimed. "Don't you see? Demetrios can't care about me. Whenever we're together something happens, something to make him turn against me. He's not that way with others; with Alexandra, he's always loving."

"That's different, Helen. She's his daughter."

"But she's not." Helen told Allison the story Mrs. Likakes had revealed to her earlier.

"So he's not Alix's father," Allison said wonderingly. "So much the better; that means he didn't love Chrysanthe."

"Not necessarily," Helen corrected her sadly. "That means Chrysanthe didn't love him. She might have turned to him in desperation, but why would he have consented to the marriage? He must have loved her secretly all the while."

"You don't know that he felt that way."

"I don't know that he didn't. It seems to explain his attitude now, why he avoids falling in love."

"Helen, Helen!" Allison exclaimed helplessly. "You two are so thick-headed and stubborn. You create obstacles. Why don't you sit down and talk? You're an English teacher and he's a psychologist and you can't find the words to communicate!" She threw up her hands in despair.

"I don't think Demetrios has anything further to communicate to me. And just to see him casually . . . I can't take it. I think I'm going back to the States, to South Elmsford."

Allison was stunned. "But why?"

"What do you mean, 'why?' It just didn't work out. I know I don't want to marry Hercules, and Demetrios has shown he doesn't care about me."

Allison grew impatient with her. "That's not reason enough. After all, you didn't come to Greece husband hunting, did you?"

Helen was indignant. "Of course not!"

"Well," Allison taunted, "why *did* you come?"

"Why . . . to teach, to change my way of life, to have new experiences and meet new people. . . ." Helen's voice was uncertain.

"That hasn't changed, has it?" Allison was unrelenting. "You have a job and, incidentally, an obligation to Jess and the school. You like the country, I know that. Be independent! Your staying shouldn't hinge only on the availability of a man to lean on. The reasons you came are good ones. Jess tells me you're a gifted teacher; we need you at the school and I know you'll like teaching there. Do some traveling before the semester starts. Be independent."

Helen was buoyed by the pep talk, but still hesitant. "I don't know; I just don't know."

Then Jess came home and the conversation stopped.

"Hey, why so serious, you two?" he asked. "Everyone's gloomy today. I just saw Demetrios when I stopped by the school for a minute and he was wandering around like a lost sheep. When I asked what was wrong I thought he'd bite my head off." Jess shook his head. "He had just said goodbye to Alix; I guess he's going to miss her."

"I guess he is," his wife agreed, "but maybe it's more than that."

"More?" Jess asked, but got no response. "Anyway," he continued, "I invited him for dinner. O.K., Al?"

Helen jumped quickly to her feet.

"Of course," Allison answered. She saw Helen preparing to leave and said quickly, "Stay, Helen. Have dinner with us."

"No, please," Helen said, feeling panicky. "Thank you, but not tonight." Despite their protests, she succeeded in getting away.

Hercules called that night and Helen welcomed the chance to solve one problem, at least. When she told him that she couldn't continue seeing him he argued with her, but less forcefully than she had anticipated.

Finally, with resignation, he agreed. "If that is really how you feel, Helen, I shall, of course, respect your wishes."

"Hercules, I believe you expected this," she said with surprise. "Did you?"

"I was concerned that your attitude was being influenced by Dr. Criades." His voice reflected his distaste. "With time, however, I had hoped that you would see that we could have a very successful marriage."

They spoke for a few more minutes and then hung up. She doubted that she would be seeing him again.

Helen went up to her room. The weather had continued hot and sultry so she left the door open, trying to create a cross-breeze. The room still felt oppressive. Perhaps she could sleep. Helen showered and scrubbed herself hard, as if to scrub away her sadness. Then she put on her coolest summer nightgown, one she had bought for her trip but hadn't worn before, brushed her hair and lay down.

But she couldn't sleep. She couldn't stop thinking of Allison's words. Her friend was right. She owed it to herself, as well as to the school, to stay, and stay she would. A sound reached her from the dark porch below. Mrs. Caratides was humming softly as she sat outside. Helen looked at her watch; it was still early, only nine-thirty. How would she get through the long night?

She would join Bertha for a while. It would be better than tossing restlessly in bed. She found a robe, put it on and immediately felt unbearably hot. She flung it off; after all, it was dark and she was covered. She went down in her nightdress.

Bertha looked up at her approach. "Welcome," she said in Greek and motioned Helen to the small settee. They sat in companionable silence. The roses in the small garden gave off their fragrance and off in the distance, Helen saw the columns of the Parthenon glowing in the moonlight. It was magnificent, but also unreal.

Suddenly she became aware of a figure moving out of the shadows. She didn't need to see him clearly; she knew it was Demetrios. She sat very still, not stirring during Mrs. Caratides's greeting or Demetrios's polite reply. She felt she hardly even breathed.

Bertha asked Demetrios to sit down. He stared hotly at Helen as he took the only available place, next to her on the settee. She looked straight ahead into the darkness.

Bertha murmured something about a cold drink and discreetly went inside, leaving them alone.

Helen tried to keep her body still as her every cell became alert to his presence, to his closeness. She sensed his anger, then heard it in his voice.

"Allison has just told me that you're thinking of leaving Greece, of returning to America."

"And if I am? Surely it's nothing to you."

"You don't know what's important to me. You have always misread what I think."

"I doubt that I've misread what you think of me. You've communicated that all right."

"And that is . . . ?"

"That I'm superficial and childish."

"And are you trying to prove me right by leaving?" he asked gruffly.

"What do you mean?"

"Behaving like a *turista* who has her summer romance and then leaves," he answered with sarcasm.

"What romance? I haven't had a summer ro- mance," she cried out in frustration, one hand clenched as if to strike out.

"Are you complaining?" he asked sardonical- ly. "Well, maybe there's still time." He pulled her to him.

She didn't want this, she told herself, not only this. She wanted so much more. She wanted him completely and forever. She would not give vent to her surging desire.

But Demetrios overcame her resistance. He pinned down her arms and kissed her lips, stifling her protests. His lips moved to her throat. She tried to fight him and as she wrenched away one of her shoulder straps broke.

When her nightgown fell to reveal a soft, white breast Demetrios groaned and lowered his lips to its taut peak. She could no longer fight him. If this was all of love she was to taste, then should she reject it? Her hand unclenched and sought his hair, caress- ingly. He raised his head and looked into her eyes.

Did he see her, or a picture of Chrysanthe? She had to know.

She pulled back, trying to cover her breast, but the bodice would not stay up unless she held it.

"You're wrong," she said, her words trembling. "I don't need your summer romance. I've decided not to leave." She heard his quick intake of breath.

"Hercules has persuaded you?" It was half state- ment, half question.

"No," she denied with spirit. "As a matter of fact, I broke up with him tonight." She peered through the darkness to read his expression.

"Then, why are you staying? Allison said that you—"

"Allison had no right to say anything to you," she interrupted.

"But she did, you little fool!" His voice was rich with emotion. "She had every right. She knows how much it means to me . . . how much you mean to me."

What was he saying? She was afraid to let herself believe, to let herself respond.

"I thought . . . the way you acted . . . Chrysanthe . . ." She broke off.

He was puzzled. "Chrysanthe? But Allison said you found out the truth, that Mrs. Likakes explained the circumstances. I'm not Alexandra's father."

"But you married Chrysanthe."

"Only to help her. She didn't know where to turn."

"I thought you may have loved her—secretly—and loved her still."

He was gently exasperated. "How wrong you were! But you could have asked me."

"You never allowed me to. When I brought up the subject you became angry. I thought you were avoiding intimacy, emotional intimacy," Helen said, blushing. "I loved you and you treated me like a child."

"I was afraid," he admitted. "Chrysanthe had been a child, squandering her emotions and then her life. If I avoided intimacy it was because you didn't seem ready to make a commitment." He reached for her again. "I was intrigued by the girl in you, her sweetness, her lovely sensuousness." He stroked her bare arm and felt her trembling response. "I couldn't resist her. I wanted to possess her." He kissed her slowly and deeply and she answered the sweet pressure. "But even more," he said against her lips, "I wanted the woman. I wanted to live with the woman I now hold."

She raised her arms to encircle his neck, oblivious to the nightgown which slipped down again. As she kissed his mouth she felt the heat of his body against her bare skin.

"Are you sure," he whispered later as he cradled her in his arms. "Are you sure you don't want to go home?"

"South Elmsford isn't really home anymore. I guess I have no home now," she said, her head against his chest.

"Here is your home," he responded softly. "Here in my arms, in this garden, in my village, wherever we are together. Here is your home."

She knew he was right. She surrendered to the magic of this realization and to the excitement of his embrace. Never had she felt so completely another's and so completely herself.

"How I want you," he whispered gruffly, "but all in due time. First the engagement, the *arevona,* then the wedding, the *gamo,* in the village and the celebration after. And then, *agape,* you and I alone together, man and wife."

"Oh, Demetrios, that sounds so long," she whispered against his lips. "Must we wait?"

"Yes, *Eleni mou.* It is the custom. Sometimes one year."

She frowned.

"Or six months."

She felt better.

"Perhaps three."

She brightened.

"It can even be accomplished in one." She kissed him. "Or less."

She abandoned herself again to his embrace. She was truly home.

READERS' COMMENTS ON SILHOUETTE ROMANCES:

"I would like to congratulate you on the most wonderful books I've had the pleasure of reading. They are a tremendous joy to those of us who have yet to meet the man of our dreams. From reading your books I quite truly believe that he will some-day appear before me like a prince!"

—L.L.*, Hollandale, MS

"Your books are great, wholesome fiction, always with an upbeat, happy ending. Thank you."

—M.D., Massena, NY

"My boyfriend always teases me about Silhouette Books. He asks me, how's my love life and natu-rally I say terrific, but I tell him that there is always room for a little more romance from Sil-houette."

—F.N., Ontario, Canada

"I would like to sincerely express my gratitude to you and your staff for bringing the pleasure of your publications to my attention. Your books are well written, mature and very contemporary."

—D.D., Staten Island, NY

*names available on request